Obsidian Tomorrow: The Storm

Obsidian Tomorrow, Volume 1

Chad Wannamaker

Published by CHADWBOOKS, 2023.

This is a work of fiction. Similarities to real people, places, or events are entirely coincidental.

OBSIDIAN TOMORROW: THE STORM

First edition. August 15, 2023.

ISBN: 978-1736591352

Written by Chad Wannamaker.

Table of Contents

OBSIDIAN TOMORROW

Chapter One:

Seattle, Washington

Black clouds sped across the sky like stampeding cattle. Heavy rain danced off awnings and building fascia. Jack tucked his chin further into the collar of his jacket as he approached the 13 Coins Bar & Grill. The subtle fragrances of rain, oily streets, exhaust fumes, and many restaurants filled his olfactory senses. The end of a long week was finding its way toward a small reward: dinner with two old friends.

Taking a moment to shake off as much water as possible, he pushed open the door and entered. A draft of warm air greeted him as he entered the restaurant. Shrugging out of his coat, he scanned the dining area and waved off the host, indicating he already had a table. Toward the back of the elaborate wood-paneled interior, he spotted Larry. Jack became enthralled by the aroma of freshly baked bread and wood-fired steak as he made his way through the crowded dining room.

Looking up, Larry flipped his hair away from his face with a shake of his head. He gave Jack a smile as he brought his beer to his lips. Wearing a rumpled white business shirt, slacks, and a loosened tie, it was apparent that Larry had come straight from work. Larry's complexion was fair, with reddish-blond hair crowning a thin face, a long nose, and a narrow mouth. His skin was mottled with light-colored stubble. Evidently, his face had missed its morning date with the razor.

"Have you been waiting long?" Jack asked.

"Nah dude. 'Got here about ten minutes ago."

Looking around the dining room, Jack said, "just you and me so far? Brad still coming?"

Larry frowned, "far as I know. You know Brad. Always on his own schedule."

Jack laughed. Brad had always done things his way, and in his own time. But he was usually on time for their monthly hangout.

"How have you been, man?" Jack asked as he grabbed a menu.

Larry smiled and shook his head. "Oh, you know. Riding the coaster and trying to predict where the market's headed."

Jack has heard all about Larry's trials with the stock market since college. Larry and his wife Natalie struggled when the financial slowdown occurred. Natalie sold real estate and was one of the more successful agents in the city. She dealt with high-end properties, but her sales were never consistent. Having to market for high-end real estate cost her monthly as well.

Trying to steer Larry onto a new subject, Jack said, "you see the news today? There's another one missing."

Larry took another large sip of his beer.

"I try to avoid hearing about any of that. Nat's obsessed with it. Thinks she's closer than the cops are to figuring out who's doing it. She's got the damn TV on the news 24/7."

The city was in a media frenzy. There had been many disappearances of young women. The Emerald City Vanishings, as it was being called, had been going on for at least two years, but no one knew when they started. To date, there were thirteen women missing, all under thirty. Several families banded together to create a website and post a reward. But they were without any leads, no ransom notes, no bodies, and very few clues.

Shrugging, Jack said, "well, it is intriguing. Makes you wonder, doesn't it?"

"No, it doesn't. My wife has cornered the market on wondering what it all means."

"Hmm...Well maybe she does. Other than that, you doing okay, Larry? I mean, other than business? You seem edgy."

Larry looked across the top of his mug at Jack. Made a grimace and said, "Nat and I had a big argument earlier. That's why I came into town. Just finished a meeting at the brokerage on my way here. I usually work out of the house on Fridays, but it was really messy."

"Sorry, man. I hope you can work it out." Jack responded, but not surprised.

Waving his empty glass at a passing server, Larry said, "Oh, sure. We always work it out. I'll have to deal with it when I get home, that's for sure."

Jack was about to suggest that Larry and Natalie think about counseling when he noticed the body language at several surrounding tables change. People were glancing in the direction of the front door.

Larry was facing the entrance and smirked at Jack.

"Did you just feel all the air getting sucked out of the room?" he laughed.

3

Looking over his shoulder, Jack recognized the huge figure clad in a leather coat, natty plaid shirt, stylish jeans, and a pair of Air Jordan 5's heading in their direction. People were doing double takes as Brad's six foot six two hundred and seventy-five-pound muscular frame smoothly navigated through the crowded dining room.

Brad smiled broadly as he saw his friends and wedged himself into the booth beside Larry.

"Let's get this party started, fellas!"

Looking at Brad with darkened eyes, Larry said, "Good evening, your Highness."

Brad glanced at Jack and Larry, "wow, I'm not that late." He leaned back and laughed.

"What held you up?" Jack asked.

Brad shrugged and said, "sometimes women don't understand I must leave now."

"Well, I hope that worked out for you."

"Always does," said Brad.

Brad looked like he always did. Upbeat, fit, and wearing his signature self-satisfied smile. But he also seemed charged up, full of extra energy.

They all had been friends since college. While Jack's career as a software programmer limped along, Brad put together a small string of gyms and spas throughout the Pacific Northwest. His vast physical stature is magnified by his confident personality and gregarious nature. Brad was good-looking but needed to be softer and more refined. He had a square jaw and prominent features. He looked like a professional football player and used that look to target women across a broad spectrum. Jack often wondered how he avoided trouble when he moved on to the next woman, which was often. He was constantly dating someone new as the previous women melted away into a blurred multiplicity of attractive faces and long legs. Brad looked across the table at Jack, with a smile full of big, straight white teeth. A long faint scar traced his jawline, curling up and ending in the cleft of his chin. It gave him a slightly dangerous look.

A tall, attractive server approached the table with Larry's fresh beer. Brad pointed at it and held up two fingers, indicating that he and Jack wanted the same. Jack smiled at the server and shook his head. He grinned at Brad's questioning glance, suggesting he was now okay.

Larry gave Jack a thinly concealed look, indicating, 'Brad's in charge...again'. Shallow-faced, and somewhat boxy in appearance; Larry was at the opposite end of the spectrum from Brad. It was a marvel how the three of them formed a bond in college since Larry was so different from the two of them.

Brad and Jack made small stock purchases with Larry's help a while ago to support their friend, but Jack hadn't pursued an extensive portfolio. As a struggling programmer, he couldn't afford to spend too much. Larry and Natalie had no kids, which Jack thought was a blessing. Larry had stumbled into the relationship and married after a short whirlwind romance. Although Natalie was beautiful, her edgy personality made it hard to picture her and Larry being romantic. Jack always expected Larry to drop the bomb and announce they were separating.

The server returned with two pints. Brad laughed, and Jack smiled, shaking his head. She apologized when Jack reminded her, he hadn't asked for one but an iced tea instead. Larry, who had already finished his beer, grabbed the pint before the server could remove it.

Brad winked at Jack as he asked for the server's number. She smiled at the charm Brad was emitting and tried to let him down nicely.

"Now, if I gave you my number, I'd have to give it to every guy that asked for it." She said, giving Brad a neutral smile.

Undaunted, Brad said, "I'm not every guy, and I've got to be at least slightly more interesting than anyone else that's asked for your number today." That earned a pity laugh as the server quickly ran through the specials, leaving them to ponder their dinner selections.

Giving his friend a leering smile, Larry raised his glass and said, "Don't you ever give it a rest? Geez! I feel like I'm on some reality TV dating show when I'm around you. Didn't you notice she pretty much blew you off?"

Brad leaned back and propped his elbows on the back of the booth, "you can't catch fish unless you're fishing."

Looking over at Jack, he said, "you aren't drinking tonight? Are you up for dinner, or will you phone that in too?"

Jack chuckled, "iced tea is a drink, and I'm ready for a good meal. I've been living off leftovers all week."

"Yeah? Under most circumstances, a beer is just a beer, but you never can tell. Having just one might change enough of what will happen around us to significantly change any of our individual destinies, potentially for the better."

Jack responded, "So, you're talking about the Butterfly effect? With a fucking beer? That's a fascinating take on an unproven theory. So, no, thank you. But I'm glad to be here."

"Well, let's enjoy ourselves. I just eliminated a huge problem and closed a deal guaranteeing enough money to finance my new location plus two more." Brad said as he smiled widely and winked at Jack while he elbowed Larry.

"That your angel investor again?" Jack asked. He and Larry had never been able to get Brad to divulge the identity of the venture capitalist who had originally staked his business. In the past, Brad had hinted that it was someone high up in local government or the financial district, but lately, he avoided discussing the topic.

Frowning for a moment and then smiling, Brad responded, "No. Fresh blood!" He laughed and raised his glass to toast his own good fortune.

The conversation segued into discussions about all their separate businesses. Brad's had money and landlord issues with his newest gym. Larry complained about his client's lack of foresight, and Jack talked about his latest project. More drinks arrived as meals were ordered, and the three spent leisurely hours enjoying dinner and passing the time.

Clearing plates later, the server asked if they were interested in dessert. Laughing and waving off any possibility of dessert Brad asked her if she'd had second thoughts about giving him her phone number.

Deliberately not looking at Brad, she made eye contact with Jack and laughed, "Is he always this aggressive? Or are you still training him how to behave in public?"

"There's no training him. We just try to stay out of the way and clean up the wreckage." Jack laughed.

Smiling, she gave Jack a second appraising glance and said, "now that, I believe. Well, at least he hangs out with quality people."

Spinning slowly on her feet, she walked away to get their check.

"Damn! What am I, grotesque or some shit?" said Larry.

"You're married man," Jack grinned as he eyed Larry's wedding band.

"Well, I mean yeah, but damn it would be nice to at least be considered," Larry said with an exasperated look.

Brad, staring at Jack open-mouthed. "Are you fucking kidding me right now? I ask for her number, and she turns to flirt with you? Wreckage? Really?"

Laughing hysterically, Larry struggled not to choke on his beer. "Bummer, dude! You went down in flames, and not a shot was fired."

Larry's drunk, shouldn't have let him grab that last beer, Jack thought to himself. During dinner, Larry continued to drink heavily, and Jack made a mental note to grab his keys if he didn't book a rideshare. Looking closely, he took in some troubling details about his friend. Always thin, Larry seemed to have lost weight. Dark circles under his eyes, heavy lines around the mouth, and a generally disheveled appearance made Larry look shabby and older than he was. This was new, or at least new, since the last time they had been out together. Maybe things with Natalie really were worse than usual. Or the market was creating severe problems for him. He watched Larry gesturing expressively as he was making some point to Brad. Laughing at Brad's response, Larry exposed his small teeth with prominent gums. That had been a familiar sight since sophomore year at Northwestern University. Jack considered taking Larry out for lunch or coffee the following week to talk about life.

"Dude, what the hell are you staring at? Have I grown a third eye or something?" Larry asked while shooting Jack a stern look.

Jack didn't realize he was staring and struggled to cover his not-so-covert inspection. "Yeah, I think it arrived right between your fourth and fifth drink. Did you drive, or did you get a ride over here?"

"Nah, I drove, but I'll probably get a ride unless one of my buddies is willing to give me a lift?"

Brad laughed and glanced at Jack because they all knew that Larry's house was out of the way for Brad and Jack. Sighing, Jack rolled his eyes. "I would, but I'm not drinking tonight because I've got to finish this site design. If I take you to the west side of town, it'll take me an extra hour to get home."

Turning an unfocused gaze on Jack, Larry feigned surprise. "Who, me, put you out? Heaven forbid that I ask my damn friends for help! I'll just shell out cab fare since my friends can't be bothered."

Jack looked at Larry amusingly, "Seriously? Reverse psychology? I don't think so."

Brad sighed and pulled out his wallet. "Here," he said as he slid a fifty-dollar bill across the table. "I've got your cab fare. Now shut up and give us a break." Brad's condo was only a few miles away, and he wanted to pre-empt any possibility that Larry might ask to stay with him.

Jack was surprised to watch Larry pocket the money without hesitation. Awkward.

The server arrived with the bill, flashed Jack another smile, and thanked them as she headed to the back of the restaurant. Brad picked up the bill and started to reach for his wallet again.

"No," Jack said. Staring intentionally at Larry, he said, "We can ALL pickup our share. Can't we, Larry?"

Pretending to be oblivious to the implied insult, Larry pulled the fifty-dollar bill from his pocket and pushed it toward the bill. "Take my share out of this."

Collecting their change and leaving a tip after some more wrangling, they all put on their coats and headed for the door. Larry pulled out his cellphone and requested a ride, much to Jack's relief.

A cold blast of wind whipped at them when they opened the door. The three huddled in the tiny entryway as they got their bearings. The rain had really started to come down in force. Reflected light smeared along the rain-washed street, bounced off cars, lamp posts, and every building surface within sight. They were about to move in the direction of Spring Street towards the rideshare pick-up bay when the door opened quickly behind them.

"Come on, fellas, pull out those umbrellas and get the hell out of the way!" said their server as she good-naturedly teased them. She gave Jack a playful shove.

She had finished her shift and was in a hurry to get to wherever she was headed. Brad was about to deliver a joke when the door flew open again as another young lady exited the restaurant. Brad, Jack, and Larry were forced into the rain with no room for such a large group in the entryway. Laughing, the two women pushed past them and ran off in the same direction the guys were walking.

All three stepped into what was now clearly a storm, a bona fide, full-tilt, Northwestern fall storm. A too-windy fall storm for umbrellas was now forcing the rain into a horizontal pattern.

"Come on! I'll have them drop you guys off at your cars, so you don't get completely soaked!" Larry shouted.

They bent their heads low to keep the rain out of their eyes as they ran up the heavily inclined street. They went with a shambling gait to avoid slipping on the wet sidewalk. Up ahead, they saw the two women slip and fall to their knees. Two unbelievably huge figures had emerged from an alley and blocked their path. Clothed in gray overcoats and with hoods pulled over their heads, the giant figures appeared faceless in the heavy rain. Moving smoothly without concern for the wet pavement, the massive figures advanced quickly like wolves. They reached down, easily picked up the women, and quickly took them into the alley. Screams muffled by the heavy rain died abruptly.

"Holy shit!" Larry screamed.

Brad began running toward the alley, with Jack following on his heels.

Larry stood flat-footed and confused. "Hey...stop! Let's call..." he pulled out his phone, hesitated for a moment then ran after Jack and Brad.

Sliding to an off-balanced stop, Brad came to the alley's mouth, and Jack nearly took him down, slipping on the slick sidewalk. The scene in the alley was so unnatural and out of perspective that it seemed surreal. Caught in the hazy glow of a dim streetlight, two monumental figures bent over the motionless woman. The heavy rain had flooded the alley. The continuing downpour slammed into the pooled water, causing a series of splashes around them. Even in a squatting position, the cloaked figures were so huge that the scene looked like adults bending over two small children. The rainfall slid off the material of the overcoats worn by the giants and seemed to leave behind a dry surface. They gave no sign of being bothered by the rain at all. One of the giant figures hunched forward as though looking for something, reaching out toward one of the motionless women.

Brad took three long strides into the alley and yelled, "Hey! You! Hold it right there! Back off!"

Larry, finally arriving at the entrance to the alley, his mouth dropped open, and he stood there holding his phone in one hand, frozen. One of the giants rose to its full height. A hooded head turned slowly toward Brad and Jack; its face hidden by a shadow. The heavy rain made the figure appear to shimmer. The other figure was still squatting over one of the women. It was grasping her coat in one huge, gloved hand and holding her chin in the other. Her friend lay on her side a few feet away, seemingly forgotten.

"I told you to BACK - THE - FUCK - OFF!" Brad roared as he rushed forward.

Jack also moved forward, drawn by the raw power of Brad's angry advance. As Brad charged, the standing giant moved to shield the other. It reached into its coat and drew out an object. In the rain, it looked like a large rock. A large volcanic rock or piece of asphalt. Jack stepped to one side, turning away from the threatening figure, attempting to divide its focus between Brad and himself. Reaching into his pocket, he felt for his phone and called 911 from voice command. Brad, who had abandoned all thoughts of caution, lowered his shoulder and launched himself at the gray giant.

Jack had seen Brad in a fight or two over the years, and he knew how to mix it up. Brad went into what he liked to call 'beast mode' when fighting. Once, he had taken on three drunks that weren't happy with how a game of pool had turned out. All three were close in size to Brad, and he had laid them out in less than a minute.

But Jack sensed that this confrontation was not going to turn out well. Brad was dwarfed by the colossal figure he was hurtling toward. Man, they were tall, Jack thought. As Brad was about to make contact, the behemoth swept out both arms, fists clenched, and let go of a swing. Its coat flapped back from the force of the blow, water spraying in all directions. The impact caught Brad high on the chest, and he flew backward as though pulled on a string. He landed on his back and slid through the flooded, trash-strewn alley before he came to a stop. He remained on his back and didn't move.

Ohh shit! Bad.

Very bad!

The first team is down! Jack thought to himself.

He glanced back to the alley entrance where Larry was still rooted, rain streaming off him. Turning around, Jack saw the giant had regrouped and was pointing the rock, holding it out at arm's length. Jack couldn't tell if he was going to throw it or...then he realized the giant was pointing the rock in Larry's direction. A muted crackling noise was accompanied by a searing bright flash as a spear of light leaped from the stone and slashed over Jack's left shoulder. The smell of ozone filled the air. The giant adroitly swept its arm, and the rock, in Jack's direction. Jack wasn't willing to go down easy and took an adrenaline-charged step toward the giant. He stared into a dark shrouded visage that was oddly familiar but alien.

"You shot my fucking friend!" he yelled.

Another flash and darkness enveloped Jack's world.

Chapter Two:

Just another day in paradise. A bright blue sky dotted with white cloud clusters stretched to the horizon to meet the brilliant blue water off Hapuna Beach. The scent of tropical vegetation hung in the humid air. Salty spray was flung high as waves crashed onto the rocks framing the beach. Daniel could feel the salt from the drying seawater crystallizing on his skin as he sat under the sun's rays.

"What haole boy? Why bodda you?" Kimmo laughed as he aimed another savage kick at the prone figure on the ground before him.

The young man tried to roll away, but Takele cut him off and threw in a vicious kick of his own. The guy had made the mistake of staring at Kimmo's girlfriend, and now he was being attacked for it. This wasn't a tourist area with Hawaiian style phony luaus, canned pineapple or little umbrellas in frou-frou drinks. This was a serious beating.

Kimmo bent over and grabbed a handful of the boy's blond hair. "So, what do you think? Maybe you shouldn't make eyes at ANY local girls, huh? Huh? You come here; you think you can steal my bitch? Huh? You fucking haole!"

Daniel looked on with growing discomfort. Haole, Hawaiian for 'white foreigner,' but in local boy parlance, 'haole' was another word for asshole, jerk, and dirtbag. Combined with the Pidgin English version of the queen mother of all profane words, that was the local salute to almost any white boy who got in the way of a kanaka and

15

his family. It wouldn't work as marketing for travel agencies. Tourists would be horrified by this ugly little secret, as they don't generally see this part of the island. But this guy had been surfing at a local beach because the resort's beaches were lousy for decent waves. He was surfing alone in an unknown area and then decided to stare at Kimmo's girl. How could he know that Kimmo was highly jealous? Kimmo once used a gravel road like a cheese grater, dragging another person's face back and forth until his friends pulled him off. That guy also had been flirting with Keone, Kimmo's girl.

All these thoughts ran through Daniel Kanahele's mind while he watched Kimmo and Takele beat the guy. Daniel thought, Keone is a major problem. She is always instigating shit just to get a rise out of him.

Daniel reached out to touch Kimmo's shoulder. "Ey, brah. Maybe you taught him enough, yeah?"

Kimmo stepped back from the now unconscious guy. He turned his head in Daniel's direction as though drunk, chest heaving from the exertion. He pushed his wet hair back out of his face.

"What? You think?" Kimmo said. His eyes narrowed as he stared at Daniel as if seeking some underhanded ulterior motive. Some trick.

After a threatening glare, Kimmo seemed to assure himself that Daniel wasn't a threat. Keone stood off to one side with her arms folded.

"My baby, you cold? Don't worry, it's good. We finished." It wasn't cold, but Keone continued to hug herself and tried not to shake.

Daniel saw the break-in activity as an opportunity to distract Kimmo and Takele enough to end the beating and save the guy's life.

"Yeah, brah, I think so. Sides, if you kill him, that's no good for nothing' bruddah." If Daniel's tutu heard him talking like this, she would beat him. She once said, 'I don't send you to a good school to hear you speaking Pidgin like those bullies at the beach.'

Kimmo looked down at the motionless body, nudging him with his foot. He jerked his head at Takele, motioning to a collection of large rocks further in the cove. Takele grabbed the guy by the ankles and dragged him over to the rocks. The rough sand scratched dozens of minor cuts into the young man's back. Finally, he pulled him up into a sitting position, propping him against a rock outcropping.

Large bruises were forming on his face and torso. Good thought, Daniel, hopefully a corpse wouldn't bruise like that. Only the living can give birth to a healthy bruise. Blood caked his hair and crusted around his nose and mouth. Daniel hoped there were no broken teeth in that mouth or any broken bones at all, for that matter. This was it. This was the last time Daniel would hang with Kimmo and Takele. It was never all that much fun under any circumstance, but they had all been friends since they could walk. Whenever Kimmo and Takele got into a bit of toking or started drinking at breakfast, it was a sure bet that the day would end badly. Add in Keone; that was like pouring gas on a bonfire. Something already dangerous and unstable was sure to get out of control.

"Yeah, well, let's get his board, drag it up here, and...what?" asked Daniel. "What are you lookin' at?"

Takele and Kimmo were standing facing Daniel. They had vacant looks on their faces, focused on something behind Daniel. Still clutching her arms, Keone looked in the same direction, but her face wasn't void of emotion or focus. Her eyes were open as wide as they could go. Daniel could see all the white around her irises, and her mouth was making an 'O'. The kind of 'O' shape that usually preceded a scream. Daniel spun around and simultaneously stepped back, almost losing his balance. Two of the largest men Daniel had ever seen approached from the direction of the beach around several large boulders. It was difficult to distinguish their features as both wore long coats. Hoods covered much of their heads. Daniel took another couple of steps backward and glanced at Takele and Kimmo. Takele was still trying to understand what it was he was seeing. But Kimmo had already decided how to react to the arrival of the two intruders. He devised a straightforward plan. Show them no fear!

"Back off! You got no business here, kapu!" he called out to the two advancing giants.

This eloquently delivered message had no effect as the massive strangers continued to stride toward them. They moved purposefully, like two hired guns moving down a quiet road toward an inevitable showdown. Kimmo bent down, grabbed several rocks, and started hurling them as hard and fast as possible.

The first one would have hit one of the strangers in the head, except he moved just enough so that it sailed past.

The second rock winged the other stranger in the shoulder, and a third found its mark hitting the first stranger on the top of his head, partially dislodging his hood. The two guys stopped. While one adjusted his hood, the other reached under his coat and withdrew a rock. The rock was dark-colored and so glossy that it almost seemed to glow and change color in the sunlight. While its shape was difficult to judge, it appeared to fit the gloved hand of the tall stranger comfortably and naturally. In an unhurried fashion, the stranger slowly extended his arm, pointing the rock toward Kimmo. Clearly not seeing the gesture as a significant threat, Kimmo laughed and said, "What? Go 'head. You think you can hit me?"

Kimmo followed up by throwing another rock at the threatening giant. The entire scene began to play out in slow motion to Daniel. The two men were at least seven feet tall and massive. Close to four hundred pounds, but not fat. Although the coats covered most of their bodies, it was clear that they were heavily muscled and likely powerful. Kimmo was barely five feet seven inches tall, and in comparison to the strange men, he looked like a Mynah bird facing off against a couple of wild boars. The rock left Kimmo's hand and was immediately shattered by a sliver of blinding light that emitted from the rock held by the giant. Pieces of rock sprayed Kimmo and Takele. Before either could do more than attempt to cover their eyes, another shaft of light leaped out and struck Kimmo in the chest, knocking him off his feet. The sharp smell of hot metal and burned flesh filled the air. A wisp of smoke curled up slowly from

Kimmo's chest as he lay sprawled in the sand, his face hidden by his hair but no doubt unconscious or worse.

Takele turned and started lumbering toward the surf. Another burst of light flashed out and struck him in the back, propelling him face first to the ground in a heap before he could reach the water.

Keone, apparently recovered from her initial shock, fulfilled the promise of her heretofore scream. The giant without the bizarre rock weapon took two long strides and, upon reaching her, tapped her on the head with two large, gloved fingers. Keone dropped to the sand so quickly that the effect was almost comical.

Funny, but not.

The weapon-wielding giant stood silently, holding the rock at his side. Small white and blue flames traced over it with subtle colors pulsing under its dark surface but causing the giant no harm.

Now Daniel stood facing the two huge strangers alone. He tried to take stock of the two figures and was confronted with one confusing detail after another. They were huge but moved fluidly, not slowly or deliberately as one would expect from men so large. The material of their clothing was unlike anything Daniel had ever seen. The coats appeared light in weight but only billowed slightly in the wind coming in from the ocean. The boots they wore were utilitarian but elegant. Indeed, they had yet to purchase anything else on the island. The gloves weren't leather but were more substantial than cloth or silk. Everything they wore was the same color, a dark gray that blended with the shadows of the lava rocks surrounding them. The two figures gave off a sense of otherness.

Daniel struggled to compose himself and meet their eyes. Hard to do when you couldn't see them hidden in the folds of their hoods as they were. "Who are you? What do you want? Why did you hurt my friends?"

Yeah, that'd show 'em. Piercing questions cleverly phrased and delivered. Now they knew they were dealing with someone who really meant business. Daniel wondered distractedly if his tutu would miss him much. He had planned on returning home in time for dinner, but things certainly hadn't been heading in that direction.

The giant who had knocked Keone out turned toward Daniel and slowly reached up to his hood. One large hand slowly pushed the hood back. Daniel found himself bracing for...what? The head that emerged from under the hood was striking in its massiveness. There was a big lantern-jawed face with heavy brows, a broad nose, and lips crowned with hair so black that when hit by sunlight, it reflected blue highlights. The eyes were deep-set and dark, with the ears hidden under long curls of hair that fell to the shoulders. The skin, the most disturbing feature by far, was ash in color and resembled the hide of a rhino. While all the elements were hauntingly familiar, they were not humanlike.

The hoodless stranger looked down on Daniel and said, "We do not submit to the will of any but the one we serve. We are here for the one who was injured." The large head turned slightly toward the still form of the unconscious guy and then turned back to Daniel.

"And we are here for you."

Shaking his head as if to clear his mind and disperse the cobwebs of a waking dream, Daniel unsteadily took a step back. "I didn't...I'm not going anywhere with you."

Ruthless dark eyes set in an inhuman face with no hint of empathy or concern looked down upon him.

"Yes. You are. Resistance is futile"

Chapter Three:

Century City, California

The sun had worked hard to cut through the late afternoon smog over the city like an old dirty, unwanted blanket. Having failed throughout the day, the oncoming sunset signaled a reluctant admission of defeat.

Several blocks from the business district, the moldering shadow of the Century Hotel huddled between a closed theater and an adult bookstore. Tired coats of paint and a sagging roof testified to better days long passed. Once occupied by aspiring stars and slumming B-list actors, the Century was now home to burnouts, addicts, and wannabe gangsters.

Rafe Pelayo watched the sunset from the window of his third-floor apartment. He would've liked to open the window to take a deep breath of fresh air and feel the breeze on his face, except the window had been painted shut years ago. There was no fresh air on the other side of the window, and the only thing Rafe might feel on his face would be the fine mist of rust and dirt that drifted off the roof 24/7. After finishing a twelve-hour shift at Tony's Tire World, 'tired' did not even come close to describing how he felt.

He had hit rock bottom and began the long slow climb back. He'd lost his house, good job, and most of his friends. Or at least the people he used to call friends. His fiancée dumped him, and he'd fallen into one situation after another with no family to fall back on. The slide had been slow at first and then picked up speed. Like watching a landslide pick up power and mass as it hurtled toward the next thing in its path. He'd messed up many things, and more than a few people had been caught in the chaos of his own personal avalanche. So, he moved through a sliding scale of jobs and places to live. It wasn't like living at home, thank God for that, even if he was often too drunk to notice most of the time. But at least he was still living on his terms. Yeah, he thought to himself, my terms. Terms with a price. He made so many compromises and concessions over the last two years that he had trouble remembering what it felt like to live in a natural home, with someone who cared about him. The last place he'd been living had been a disaster. Five roommates, a communal bathroom, and funky social dictums that he couldn't deal with anymore. It all seemed promising at first, but the novelty wore off quickly.

The Century could have been a better place by any standard, but the rent was cheap, he was close to work, and no one was trying to get into his business.

Rubbing his jaw and feeling the stubble growing since that morning, Rafe weighed his choices for the evening. Crappy TV on his even crappier television downing beers, eating dinner alone at Baller's Burgers, or calling Brenda. The call to Brenda wasn't a real option because she was still pissed over their last weekend together. Tony's Tire World had commandeered Rafe's, and by association, Brenda's, Friday night schedule. Brenda has acted differently since. So, a choice between a greasy dinner with some cold ones or bad TV and whatever was left in the fridge. At least Rafe didn't have to worry about roommates. He has been down that road and was glad to be done marking his food with a Sharpie.

His phone buzzed on the kitchen counter, and Rafe shuffled to answer. The caller ID announced 'BRENDA' was calling. Rafe swiped to answer as fast as he could.

"Hey," he rasped.

Silence on the other end was finally broken with, "So, why haven't you called me about getting together tonight?"

Rafe sighed. "Aren't you still mad?"

"No."

"Well, I thought you were."

"Well, I'm not."

Wow, this is really going great, he thought to himself.

"I called six times, and Christine said you were too busy to come to the phone."

Rafe heard a petulant huff on the other end of the phone.

"Well, I WAS mad, but now I'm not."

"So, do you want to hang out?"

"No, but I want to GO out," Brenda said with a huff.

Rafe had experienced this little verbal dance with Brenda so often that he could practically carry both sides of the conversation alone. The only problem was he was too damn tired to feel up to it, especially after she'd left him wondering all week. He was about to tell her how he felt when someone knocked with thunderous authority on his door.

"Hang on, someone's at the door."

"Do you have a bitch there with you?"

"What? No! Just hang on! Geez." Rafe moved toward the door and walked up to the security peephole. This was a handy little feature Rafe had installed himself just days after moving in and discovering how sketchy his neighbors were. Leaning forward toward the lens, Rafe jumped back when another loud, forceful knock shook the door.

"Hey! Cut the shit! Who is it?" Rafe's heart started hammering in his chest. He hadn't been able to see through the peephole. Was it a debt collector? None of his few friends would belligerently pound on his door. Not this loudly or powerfully.

He spoke urgently into the phone.

"Brenda, stay on the line and get ready to call 911 if something happens to me."

"Something... something like what? Listen, Rafe, are you in trouble?"

"Just shut up and wait, okay?"

"Don't you tell me to shut up, asshole!"

Another massive blow crashed into the door.

"You do that again, and I'm calling the cops, fucker!" Rafe hung up on Brenda and started dialing emergency. He could feel sweat forming under his arms. His hands felt cold and clammy.

Retreating slowly from the door, Rafe put the phone to his ear.

"911. Please state the nature of the emergency."

Rafe watched as the door to his apartment began to bow inward. A colossal weight slowly pushed the door in; the frame began popping away from the wall. The deadbolt strained, bent, and then snapped off sideways. The

26

doorknob tilted toward the doorjamb, and then the frame cracked.

"I'm being attacked. Somebody's breaking down my door. I don't have anything to..." The door completed its escape from the door frame, dropped one inch to the floor, and started falling inward. "...oh, God!"

Rafe knew nothing good could come from the other side of the door; voice cracking, he spoke into the phone.

"You better get here right away! I NEED SOME FUCKING HELP!"

The figure standing in the hallway was immense. The face was only partially visible because it was too tall for the doorway. As it stooped to enter, a hood fell back from the head, revealing a completely alien and yet familiar countenance. Rafe knew he'd seen the face or one like it before but couldn't place it.

Finding his voice, Rafe stammered, "I've called the police! They'll be here any second! You better get back and leave before they get here! I'll press charges!"

Yeah, as though this freak would care about that.

The bluntly chiseled, gray face bent slowly to look directly at Rafe. Coal-black eyes stared at him from beneath rugged heavy brows. A massive, gloved hand reached under the long coat and emerged, holding a large smooth stone. Polished and dark, it seemed like glass; colors swirled and moved beneath its surface.

The intruder spoke, "No one will arrive in time. We have come for you."

As he spoke, another giant stepped in from the hall. Rafe now faced two ridiculously huge creatures that, while not human, were so humanlike that the differences and similarities were confusing. And how was it that something that looked like this could speak?

Rafe took an involuntary step backward.

"You're here for me? I don't know what you want me for, but I'm not going without a fight."

Swallowing hard, he bent his knees and braced for the rush he felt was coming next. Still holding the phone in his right hand, he could hear a faint voice saying something about keeping the line open.

Big ugly number one seemed to be looking at the phone and slowly and ponderously shrugged his massive shoulders. "You cannot prevail."

That was arrogant of it to say but probably true, all things considered.

Rafe felt his stomach churn with an overload of adrenaline. Grasping at any flimsy means of creating a distraction, he drew his arm back, intending to hurl his phone at the closest stranger.

With an impossible speed for a large being, the giant swiftly and smoothly pointed the black stone at Rafe. A brilliant flash exploded around the rock, a sparkling light needle reached out and slammed into Rafe's chest, and then...oblivion.

Chapter Four:

Seattle, Washington

Larry left the cab, paid the driver, and walked the last two blocks to his house. What time is it anyway? Glancing at his watch, he winced when he realized it was almost three in the morning.

The cops had been ridiculous. That asshole Wilkes had been the worst. How often did you have to say 'I don't know' before they realized you didn't know!

The cops initially focusing on him and Brad for the mugging and disappearance of the young woman was beyond stupid. If the other woman hadn't regained consciousness and adamantly sworn that the assailants couldn't have been Larry and Brad, they would be in county lock up. They'd even taken his damn shirt!

He turned the corner and cut through a neighbor's property to get to the gate leading to his backyard. Closing the gate quietly behind him, he went to the enclosed patio and let himself into the house through the French doors. He took a deep breath, let out a long sigh, and struggled to keep his balance. Must have had a few too many, he thought to himself.

Flipping on lights as he went inside, he headed to the kitchen. There was a strong, pungent odor permeating the house. Smelled like wet metal or rust. His head pounded from the heavy drinking earlier.

No noise from upstairs. No surprise there.

He would have to go up there eventually, sort things out, and figure out what to do. Maybe later. There isn't any rush. Plenty of time for that later.

Humming absentmindedly as he moved around the kitchen, Larry pulled a half-eaten pie from the refrigerator, grabbed a fork from a drawer, and sat at the kitchen table. Pulling the plastic wrap off the pie as he started to eat.

Cherry. My favorite.

Too early to call it breakfast, and too late to call it a midnight snack. Somehow that struck Larry as very funny, and he started to laugh. Too bad he'd have to head upstairs later and deal with the mess.

That would be a downer, but not right now. Larry could figure that out later.

Chapter Five:

Seattle, Washington

The wind caressed the red maple trees outside Brad's apartment, spinning leaves and branches in a lazy ballet. Seeing the trees moving about while the thick walls and insulated windows shut out all outside noise was disconcerting. With the right music, it might seem like the maples were moving and swirling to some classical arrangement. The low, early morning sun is hidden behind dark layers of cloud.

Rain for sure, Brad thought.

Maybe a storm.

Having finished his workout in his private gym, Brad went about the rest of his morning routine with a distracted air. Walking through the luxurious sitting room, he went into his gourmet kitchen. Passing a full-length mirror in the master bedroom hallway, Brad gave himself a quick appraising glance. Bulging biceps, shredded abs, and ripped quads. Everything was in order here, he congratulated himself. The self-inspection was over almost before it started, and he mentally moved on to the next need. Time for some eggs, he thought. He had gotten home late after the fiasco at the police station and was starving.

He called Jack's phone around three in the morning and went to bed shortly afterward. He replayed the events in his mind dozens of times. The entire experience was so bizarre and unreal. The police had even confiscated Larry's shirt so they could analyze the damage to it. That was bizarre.

Larry had been vaguely aware that he had been shot with some sort of weapon, but he suffered no unpleasant effects. Other than losing consciousness and suffering some bruises and scrapes from the fall. His shirt hadn't been so fortunate. The front it looked as though it had been soaked in bleach and was brittle to the touch. It was taken away after the paramedics cut it off to examine him. After a quick examination revealed no significant concerns, Brad and Larry were taken to the Seattle Police Department's precinct on Virginia Street.

Once there, their stories were repeated to the cops several times. Brad had tediously recounted every detail over and over. Detectives Fisher and Wilkes had caught the case because it was labeled a possible homicide. Fisher handled the questioning of Brad, while Wilkes handled Larry. The questioning progressed from cordial to professional and was very thorough. After a break for coffee, the interrogation took a decidedly nasty turn.

Brad hadn't realized then that Larry had been doing his best to irritate the detective interrogating him in the next room. Larry had an almost supernatural ability to get under anyone's skin quickly. Larry had made Fisher mad enough to throw a coffee mug across the room. And as a result, what should have taken an hour or maybe less turned into a six-hour marathon. It finally ended when the other young woman, who had been knocked out, convinced them that Brad and Larry had nothing to do with the assault. They were advised that they should stay in town should further questioning be needed. Then they were released.

Just like Larry to screw shit up by being belligerent, Brad thought.

Now here he was, trying to put his day together, and he had to worry about the police likely bringing him back into the mess because Jack was still missing. And the server for that matter. Why would they both be gone? That had been the biggest issue for the police. And who or what were those huge muggers? Brad had never experienced anything like this and struggled to figure out how to move forward.

He still had some problematic business issues with the new gym and the funding he secured. He didn't have time for all this. The biggest obstacle in his personal and professional life had been resolved the day before. Brad congratulated himself on closing that door.

A chime sounded announcing that someone was wanting to be buzzed in from the ground floor reception. Brad walked over to the monitor on the wall by the front door. He saw detective Wilkes shifting uncomfortably from one foot to the other, standing outside the front door of the building in the cold breezy weather.

It was too early for the doorman to be on duty. Pressing the button to release the lock four stories below, Brad said, "Come on up."

Detective Wilkes made his way into Brad's apartment a few minutes later, looking cold, grim, and irritated.

Attempting to start on a cooperative note, Brad motioned him into the living area and invited Wilkes to make himself comfortable. Wilkes walked into the room with a stiff-legged stride without removing his coat.

Taking a seat in an oversized, overstuffed chair, Wilke's jaw popped as he spoke in a raspy voice.

"I understand you went through a long evening, but if you can answer a few questions, I'll be out of here quickly."

"Don't you guys usually do this in pairs?" asked Brad, sitting on the couch facing the chair, a low table separating them.

Wilkes exhaled noisily, "No, we usually follow up leads together, but the Q & A legwork goes faster if we split up."

"So, what's going on? Have you got any new information?"

Hunching forward, Wilkes ignored the question and looked hard at Brad, "Why would your friend give us the wrong address for his house?"

That caught Brad off guard.

"Larry? What address did he give you?"

"515 Cherry Street in Woodinville." Wilkes continued to glare at Brad with a cynical smile playing on his face.

"Do you know how much I like driving an hour and a half out of my way only to find someone's not shooting me straight?"

Brad was at a loss.

"I don't know his street address, but he lives in West Seattle, over the bridge. Driftwood Lane, maybe? I don't know why he would give the wrong address. It could be a mistake someone made when taking his information."

"That would be me, and I didn't make a mistake when I wrote it down." Wilkes was clearly trying to exert some self-control, and he was clearly having trouble being successful. "You don't know his street address? What about through social media? Or an e-mail account? Would you be able to pull it up that way?"

Brad irritably ran a hand through his hair. "Yeah, but it might take me a few minutes."

"I'll wait," said a clearly irritated Wilkes.

Ten minutes later, Brad had managed to dig Larry's address out of some old e-mail files.

"Officer Wilkes..."

"Detective, actually."

"Okay, Detective...have you tried calling Larry? I mean, last night was just fucking weird. He may have been so rattled that he just gave you the wrong address."

The disgusted look on Wilkes' face spoke volumes.

"No, I don't think he was 'rattled.' He was having fun being very uncooperative. Deliberately providing fraudulent information during an investigation is a problem. An investigation involving assault possible kidnapping or murder is serious business. And, yeah, we've tried to reach him. He's not answering his phone. It rings and goes to voice mail."

Brad looked at Wilkes and took stock. This guy's attitude was starting to seriously piss him off. Here was a guy in his fifties, in pretty good shape, getting closer to getting his pension and calling it a career. Then he deals with Larry's shit, and now he can't find him. He's tired and put out. As much as he rubbed him the wrong way, Brad figured there was no point in letting the situation get out of control. As much as he hated cops, he forced himself to relax and decided to take another approach.

"Look, detective, why don't we try to start over here? I'm interested in the same things you are, so if we can work together amicably, we may create positive momentum."

"You and your friend are still Persons of Interest, so, let's keep it formal, shall we? My partner still likes you and your buddy for the mugging. Not as the persons committing the assault but as the 'ropers' or 'stringers.' This means that you two herded the women toward two other accomplices. The faster we run down all potential leads, the better."

Brad could feel the blood rushing up to his cheeks. This guy was really pushing. He had half a mind to kick him out and be done with it. He clenched his fists and took a breath.

"Okay. I get it. You weren't there, so our stories must sound ridiculous. Larry can be a real asshole. Believe me, I know. So, I will do my part to cooperate and be part of the solution instead of being part of the problem. So, what's next? You said you had questions. Is there something else? Or was tracking down Larry the whole deal? And if that's all of it, why would that include me? And why are you trying your best to piss me off? Why is this such a big deal? I got mugged. Aren't you guys busy chasing after all those missing women anyway?"

Wilkes stood, took off his damp jacket, and sat back down after carefully folding it over the back of the chair. He cocked his head to one side and seemed to come to a decision.

"That's not amusing, so I will ignore that as you blowin' off steam. You were messed up last night, so let's start over. Your buddy, on the other hand, seems like a serious problem. My partner likes you two for the mugging. I don't. You guys and the girl are out cold; everybody else goes missing. So, where's your buddy and the other girl? Why are you knocked out and left behind? Why take your buddy and the girl? Sex trade? Robbery? None of that tracks for me. The longer the two of them are missing, the more likely they'll turn up dead, or never be found. If the girl hadn't had the same goofy descriptions, you and Ellsworth had given, you'd still be downtown explaining things. So, Ellsworth isn't where he said he'd be this morning, which means your friend is hiding something. And that makes you both look bad. People don't forget their home addresses, particularly when they are enough on the ball to be articulate and a wiseass at the same time. He might not be covering anything up case related, but your guy is a loose end. So, you with me so far?" Wilkes concluded.

"Yeah, I hear you," Brad responded tersely.

Wilkes took a breath through his teeth and smiled. "Okay. Here are my other questions: first, have you had any contact with Larry Ellsworth today?"

"No."

Wilkes grunted but seemed to believe that. "Well, I will ask for your help on something else here in a minute. Second, does this look anything like the two thugs who you ran into?" he asked as he pulled a folded piece of paper from his shirt pocket and reached out to hand it to Brad.

Unfolding a fax transmission of a charcoal sketch, Brad looked at it closely. He felt there was a resemblance but not enough to say that it matched either of the things that had attacked them. Still, the drawing evoked some memory.

Wilkes picked up on the flicker of interest.

"What? You see something?"

"No. Well, yes, sort of..." and then it hit him. He knew where he'd seen the faces before. Embarrassment came over Brad, and he felt flush again.

"Then what? Do you know them? The drawing's a match? What?" Wilkes implored, leaning forward, elbows on his knees.

Clearing his throat, Brad said, "Something. I don't know. Well, I do, but...I don't want to say. It's crazy. I've been describing all sorts of weird shit, and I don't want to add one more comment to your file on me and get myself labeled as questionable."

"Too late for that, but I'm one of the few that thinks you're probably being truthful, so give it up. Trust me," encouraged Wilkes.

Shaking his head, Brad looked at Wilkes with a grimace.

"I've been wondering why I've had this feeling that I've seen these guys before. This drawing, where did you get it?"

"My old partner works for Century City PD. A desk clerk at a rundown hotel in Century saw two big guys come in last night. This wouldn't typically be any big deal except that they were huge, and there was an abduction that followed their appearance. His description was initially written off, but the guy got a decent look at them. He seemed to be genuinely freaked out. My buddy was telling me about it this morning on the phone, and it seemed too much of a coincidence to ignore. We compared notes. The sketch was drawn by a police artist. So, what do you remember?"

Brad sighed and leaned back against the couch, anger evaporating, feeling deflated and suddenly tired.

"I think I know why I remembered seeing these guys."

"You're really making me work for it here. Would you spit it out? What can be crazier than what you three said last night?"

Rubbing his face with both hands, Brad decided to blurt it out.

"Easter Island. The guys I saw last night reminded me of those huge head statues from Easter Island."

Wilkes slumped back in his chair and looked at the ceiling.

"Don't say that to me."

"Hey, you think I want to come off sounding like some fuckin lunatic. I didn't even want to say it myself!"

"I can't, and I mean CANNOT take that to my superiors. I like my job, and I'm not getting reassigned at my age because I started buying into that kind of shit. Fisher and I are already getting crap from the rest of the station about last night. I can't add this to it. I won't. Try again."

Brad pulled his hands away from his face and glared at Wilkes.

"No. It was hard enough saying it the first time, but I'm not taking it back either. Easter Island. That's my final answer."

Wilkes started appraising the virtues of the ceiling again and let out an explosive sigh.

"What the fuck, man!"

Chapter Six:

A hazy mental fog lifted as Jack struggled to get his bearings. Shaking his head to clear the disorientation, he felt the warm floor beneath him. He was lying on his side, slowly recalling the mugging, the largest men he had ever seen, and the black rock. Jack sat up. Realizing he wasn't home or anywhere recognizable, he got to his feet, still light-headed and confused. As his sight cleared, the unmistakable outlines of several bodies were scattered around him.

Taking in his surroundings, Jack noted the walls, floor, and ceiling were all the same muted color of golden brown. Everything seemed to blend except for the dark pink leather couches and chairs scattered around.

What is that all about? Jack thought.

The room was pleasantly lit with light that came from torches placed in wall sconces at random intervals. As he looked closer, he could see that the torches were artificial. There was one door and no windows. The door was set flush with the wall and appeared impossible to open or close. It was hard to figure out the ceiling height because it was so high.

Jack heard a weak groan behind him.

What was that?

He turned around and saw one of the people roll over and sit up. To his surprise, it was the server from the restaurant. He bent down and offered her a hand to help her up.

She instinctively accepted his hand, and then, looking up, her eyes went wide with vengeful recognition.

"YOU!" she screamed and landed a glancing blow to Jack's chest, missing his face.

Staggering backward in surprise, Jack raised a hand to ward off another swing.

"Hey! Easy! What the fuck are you hitting me for?"

"You attacked me you piece of shit! What do you want from me?"

"No, I didn't. We're in the same boat here. I mean, we tried to save you. You and your friend."

"You what?"

"Yeah, remember the big guys chased you? We followed and tried to help you two."

"Yeah. Okay...Okay," she said, more to reassure herself than to offer Jack any confidence that she wouldn't try to hit him again.

"Hey, seriously, are you okay?" Jack said in a calmer tone.

"Yeah, I think so. I mean I feel okay, just confused."

"Great, I'm okay too. At least I think I am. And would you stop trying to hit me, please?"

The server, flipping her long black hair away from her face, stepped back and tried to compose herself.

"Okay, but if you're lying to me, no promises."

Jack gave a slight chuckle, "Well if that's all I can get, I'll take it."

She looked at Jack, with a softer look, trying to judge his trustworthiness. Letting out a soft sigh, she gave a slight shudder.

"Cheyenne? Is she here too?" She asked.

They both turned together, scanning the other people in the room, looking for her friend. She was not one of the other people lying on the floor around them.

She looked back at Jack. Doubt still flickering in her eyes.

"Where's your friend? Friends? What in the hell is going on!?"

"Take it easy. I don't know what happened to us or my friends. My name's Jack. You and your friend were leaving the restaurant, and we saw you getting attacked. We tried to come and help. I got knocked out and woke up here just like you." Jack said, taking a step back, putting a hand outward to stop more attacks.

"Yeah, okay. I remember...some of it. You and your friends were at the Coins, and we saw you outside before the...but...what happened? Where are we? And why are we here...why are you here, wherever here is? What is this place?" the young woman said, rubbing her shoulder.

She turned around again, slowly taking in the sparse details that Jack had been taking note of moments before.

Reasonably good questions, Jack thought to himself.

Kidnapped? Yeah.

Hostage situation? It felt like it was different.

Ransom? Unlikely.

Jack didn't know the circumstances of the others, but he didn't have anyone willing or able to pay money for his return. The room, unornamented and straightforward in appearance, hinted at power and wealth of some kind. So, what then? There was an element of the unknown, especially since the gigantic men that had attacked them were so odd. This fact made any guessing seem like a waste of time. Jack looked at the figures around him. Three men and one woman. The men appeared of different ethnic backgrounds. Two white and one brown skinned. All looked to be in their twenties or early thirties. Two of the men had on shorts without a shirt. The woman had dark skin and was older than all the others.

Do the differences between them mean anything? Still disoriented, Jack turned to look at the young woman beside him. She was tall and well-toned. She was gorgeous, even as disheveled as she was. Dark hair fell well below her shoulders. She had a pale complexion and beautiful green eyes.

"What's your name?" Jack asked.

Snapping out of her own internal contemplation, she looked up at him. "Uhh, Madeline Bamford. Maddy."

"Nice name. I'm Jack Ellington. And Jack isn't short for anything." He said with a smile.

"Hmm, what's all over your shirt?" her eyes focused on his chest.

Jack looked down at his shirt and saw a white powdery stain all over the front of his shirt. Whatever it was hadn't gotten onto his jacket. He brushed at the spot, and his shirt crumbled beneath his hand. Trying not to panic, he pulled up his shirt and felt his chest. Nothing.

What is going on? Is this where I got shot?

Then he remembered his phone. He quickly took it out, but there was no service.

Taking her cue from Jack, Maddy pulled out her phone from her coat pocket. It was the same. She had power but no signal.

He looked from her to the people on the floor and back.

"I can't figure out what's going on. Me being here, you...my shirt. And this room seems like a scene out of a horror movie. It's just too much of something...normal and strange at the same time. Like the door and the torches. It might just be some new fiber optic technology, but I've never seen anything like them."

Excellent, Jack. Very informative. So intelligent and analytical. If she didn't think you were a idiot before, she will now.

Giving the door and torches another look, Maddy shook her head.

"Why? Who would do this?"

When Jack shrugged, she looked at the others on the floor and started walking toward the woman.

"Do you think they're hurt? I mean, seriously injured?"

"I don't think so, but maybe we should check." He said as he bent down and reached out to the man lying closest to him. Clothed only in board shorts, early twenties, tan, fit. He touched the man's shoulder and gave it a gentle shake. No response. The man's chest was rising and falling regularly, so he was alive. Under different circumstances, Jack would just assume he was sleeping. He gave the man's shoulder another nudge again, still waiting for a response. Jack leaned in for a closer look at the unresponsive man. His face looked fresh, scrubbed, and healthy. His hands were smooth and clean.

Maddy knelt by the woman, gently touching her face, no response. Jack wondered why he and Maddy were awake, and they were still unconscious. Did that mean they had arrived first? Or that they were more important than the others? Come to think of it, he really didn't feel any aches or discomfort. He remembered Brad had been thrown through the air and landed on his back. If Jack had been hit similarly, wouldn't he feel at least a little sore?

He stood up, walked over to the door and pushed gently against it. Nothing. He pushed harder, again nothing. Running his hand along the very narrow seam around the door, he could not figure out how to open it. It could be a line carved into the wall in the general shape of a door. The wall and the pseudo door were the same. Dimensions of the door were massive. It was roughly ten feet high by the seven-feet wide.

"'Ey, what the heck?" Jack turned to see one of the men sitting up, looking at him with a dazed expression on his scruffy face.

"Where the fuck...what the...what is goin' on here?" He turned his head, taking in the room.

Jack walked over to him and extended his hand, offering him help to get to his feet. He grabbed Jack's hand with suspicious hesitation and got to his feet.

"Thanks."

"No problem. I'm Jack." Jack pointed over his shoulder at Maddy.

"That's Maddy. We both got mugged in an alley and woke up here. What happened to you?"

Running his hands through his long frizzy hair, the young man looked around the room again and stopped when his eyes locked on the unconscious, partially clothed young man.

"Oh, damn! My name's Daniel. Daniel Kanahele. I got shot by two guys while I was at da beach with some friends." He said as he quickly looked around the room again, as if looking for someone else.

"Yeah? Well, the way you and he..." still unconscious, Jack pointed at the board-short-wearing young man, "...look, you must have been on the same beach. We got jumped in Seattle at night, in the middle of a storm. What beach were you on?"

While stretching his arms and legs, Daniel stopped, expressing surprise, and responded with a question, "Seattle? Seattle, Washington?"

Maddy rolled her eyes. "Yes. Seattle, Washington."

Smiling, Jack answered ruefully, "Is there another? Yeah, man. Washington state. You?"

"Hapuna Beach. Close to Waimea on the Big Island." Seeing Jack's confusion, he elaborated, "The big island of Hawaii."

Her eyes widening, Maddy stammered, "Did you say Hawaii?"

Jack was stunned. Hawaii? How had they been brought here? By plane, boat? And how long had they been out? Was this place closer to Seattle or Hawaii? He looked Daniel over from head to toe. No shoes, just the shorts tied off with a drawstring. No shirt. Skin the color of caramel, long hair, and wispy facial hair that looked like a terrible decision not to shave for a few days. So, Daniel was Hawaiian. And he seemed to know the guy on the other side of the room, but apparently wasn't overly concerned about his wellbeing. He almost seemed afraid to look at him.

"So, do you know that guy? Was he one of the friends you were with at the beach? What about them," Jack asked pointing at the woman and man lying near the corner of the room furthest from the door, where they were gathered.

Hanging his head, then looking back up to meet Jack's gaze, Daniel said, "Nah. I don't know them, but the haole there..." he pointed out the board short man Jack had indicated, "... he's not my friend, but he was at the beach. My friends were giving him a beating before...before those monstrosities showed up and things got pupule."

Raising his eyebrows, Jack asked, "what purple monstrosities?"

Daniel sighed, "No man, freaks. Crazy, dude. Just crazy."

"Crazy?" Maddy asked. "What's crazy?"

Jack looked at Maddy, who had removed her coat and placed it like a blanket over the unconscious young man.

"Why were your friends beating on him?" Jack asked as he looked over at the guy still on the floor. The young man didn't seem injured. Was his unconscious state due to the beating or something else random in this nightmare?

Looking from Maddy to Jack, Daniel chuckled, "Crazy? This is all pupule, yeah? Why was Mr. Resort-living, richie-haole-boy getting his ass kicked? 'Cause he was in the wrong place at the wrong time. 'Cause he didn't know better than to flirt with a complete psycho's girlfriend. 'Cause he had the nerve to live a better life than my brahs and rubbed it in their face. You see? He didn't know where he was and who had the mana. Maopopo? Understand? And speaking of crazy...where the hell are we?"

Maddy took a deep breath, "you're saying they were beating him just because? Because he wandered into your turf? And he made a pass at your friend's girl? And you end up here with us? We're victims! We got mugged! I don't get this; it's all such bullshit!"

Jack reached out to calm her, but she pulled away, walked over to a couch, and sat down. Leaning back into the couch, she crossed her arms over her chest and glared at the door. Jack thought that while she had reason to be angry, they may have been missing something more important here.

"You said you got shot, and things got crazy. Crazy how?" Jack asked.

"Hey, dude, I don't know you, and I just woke up. You got a head start here, so tell me what you and your girlfriend saw first."

"She's not my girlfriend. We're not together. Okay, I'll go first and tell you what happened to me. But first, I have just one question about you and your friends attacking that guy. Was it you and your buddies, or just your buddies?"

"Just Kimmo and Takele. And you'll have to take my word for it, but I was there, and I'm not proud. I got 'em to stop before they killed him, but I shoulda done more. You know, yeah?" Staring at his shoeless feet, Daniel was visibly embarrassed and remorseful. Jack believed him.

"Look, let me tell you how Maddy and I got here, and then, if you don't think I'm nuts, you can tell me your crazy story. Okay? Then maybe we can figure out how to get out of here."

"Sure, dude. But you might get more than you 'spect, yeah?"

Jack took a breath and was about to share the events leading up to his awakening in the room when he heard Maddy gasp. Spinning quickly to look at her, he saw Maddy shakily stand up, holding her arm out in front of her. She was pointing at the door behind Jack and Daniel.

The door was moving.

Chapter Seven:

Waimea, Hawaii

Gray clouds filled the late afternoon sky as the sun edged closer to the horizon. The October Ocean scooped small cliffs out of the sandy beach as the strengthening tide continued its evening retreat. Tropical smells that had been so strong during the day's heat were now dominated by the smell of the surf and approaching rain. It could be seen far off in the distance. Birds that had been flying about looking for food minutes before were now scarce as they sought shelter, anticipating the evening wind.

Kimmo was smiling and lying through his teeth. His skin started to itch from all the dried sea salt and sand. A slight chill was in the air, and the cops were seriously about to make him angry. Keone was already pissing him off because she wouldn't stop crying. But, at least, she was smart enough to keep her mouth shut. Takele, well, Takele was trying to be the best Takele he knew how to be. At that moment, that meant being quiet as he was struggling to understand the nuances of the conversation unfolding before him. Kimmo could tell Takele was preparing to contribute to the discussion, which would be a disaster. The last time Takele tried to be clever, he nearly electrocuted himself while trying to fix the TV and, in the process, burned some of the house. He took the back of the TV off and started poking around in it with a screwdriver...while it was plugged in. The TV caught fire, and the house began to burn. When Kimmo got home and met the fire department in the driveway. He wanted to know why Takele had been messing with the TV. 'But brah, it was broken, and I was missin' my favorite show!' Takele opined.

Now here they were, up in the parking lot overlooking Hapuna Beach, being questioned by the cops. Clouds were rolling in, the surf was starting to kick up, and he was missing it. All because some nosey keikis had seen the whole thing going down with the haole, and their parents had called the cops. Kimmo needed to keep talking so that Takele didn't feel inspired to start adding to the story.

"Yeah, so we just catchin' waves, you know? And then we saw these big buggies beating the shit out this haole boy, so we tried to break it up. But those buggies knocked us out, brah. Next thing we know, everyone's gone." Kimmo smiled at the two uniformed officers. He mentally congratulated himself for laying off the whole thing on the freaks that had shown up. Someone else had to have seen them because they were so huge.

The bigger of the two cops, Rodillas, cocked his head sideways as he stared at Kimmo.

"That's your story? The kids said they saw three of you beating on some haole while she..." he nodded at Keone, "...stood and watched. They didn't say anything about two big guys; you're the only one saying that."

The other cop, Yoshioka, observed Keone's and Takele's reactions.

"That what the two of you saw?"

Keone nodded, trying to wipe her tears with the back of her hand. Takele glared back at the cops without answering.

"Yeah, that's what they saw. That's what happened." Kimmo said quickly. He was worried because Takele looked dangerously close to saying something stupid.

Turning and putting a hand on Kimmo's chest, Yoshioka shoved him back several steps.

"I'm not talking to you, asshole."

The ingratiating smile on Kimmo's face disappeared in a heartbeat. His mouth went tight, and his brows furrowed like a thunder cloud warning of an advancing storm. Nobody talked to him that way. Least of all, some stupid cop. He thrust out his jaw and asked,

"Ey brah, you like go?"

Takele took one lumbering step toward Yoshioka but was brought up short by Rodilla's hand. "Stay put, fat boy. Nobody wants your help since you can't speak for yourself."

Positioning himself so that his right shoulder faced Kimmo squarely, Yoshioka replied,

"What? With you... or your girl?" He leered at Keone.

His eyes bugging and mouth hanging open in disbelief, Kimmo charged the officer. Yoshioka, a broad five feet ten inches, swung the Maglite he was holding in his left hand as he parried Kimmo's rush. The heavy flashlight caught Kimmo dead center in the solar plexus, and he crumbled to the ground. Struggling to catch his breath, Kimmo writhed on the ground, grabbing his chest with both hands. Rodillas moved forward, knelt, and cuffed him with no wasted motion.

Watching in disbelief, Keone dropped to her knees on the asphalt, covering her mouth with her hands. Takele decided that he needed to do something. For the second time that day, he exercised more intelligence than anyone who knew him would expect. He slowly raised his hands over his head. And kept them there until Officer Yoshioka pulled them down one at a time while he put on the cuffs.

Chapter Eight:

Seattle, Washington

As the morning turned into afternoon, the wind picked up. The gentle breeze stirring the leaves in a slow dance outside Brad's condo was replaced by a new choreographer. This brought on the shaking of branches and whipping about of leaves. The dark clouds that had been threatening all morning began to pelt the windows with the first drops of new rain. The condo's adaptive thermostat sent an electric current through the windows to keep them from fogging and lit the gas-powered fireplace.

Wilkes got off the phone after bringing his partner up to speed. He gave Fisher Larry Ellsworth's address, but he left out the crazy Easter Island comment. Fish was tired of all the components of this case, and he wasn't even sure if he was being screwed with. This whole mess was all crazy. Wilkes stared at Brad for several seconds, trying to judge whether he was being baited or not. He hated being jerked around.

"You really going to stick with that story? Easter Island? You prepared to swear to that in a deposition?"

Brad looked at him, "Hell no. I'm just telling you. You ask me to offer any more eyewitness stuff that will be written down; I'll just say it was dark, and I couldn't see well with the rain."

"The rain," Wilkes repeated sarcastically. "That's perfect. Why tell me anything? Why not just tell me they were aliens. Yeah, that's it. Right out of Star Wars or Star

Trek. And we can't find enough evidence to corroborate your account because they just beamed up to the Bird of Prey and got the hell out of there!"

Groaning with exasperation, Brad spat out,

"No evidence? What about Larry's shirt? What was that all about? What is your special team, your CSI guys telling you about that shit? Would you just give it a fucking rest? I'm trying to help, and if you keep pushing me, you can just get your ass out of here. That's really what they looked like. I mean, look at that sketch. You can see a little of what I'm talking about in some of those features. Show that damn desk clerk some photos of those monoliths from Easter Island and see what he says. Would you rather I hadn't said anything? Where does that get me or you, for that matter?"

Wilkes grunted cautiously and looked at the sketch. Maybe.

Clearing his throat, Wilkes decided to press on.

"Yeah, well, we'll come back to that later. And as far as your buddy's clothes go, maybe he doesn't know how to do laundry. You're right, I'll bring it down a notch because you are cooperating, and trust me, not everybody does. So, let's see how much you can help me on something else. Are you willing to make a phone call?"

Brad could see where this was headed. "To Larry? Yeah, I guess. But if you're not getting any answer, do you really expect him to pick up for me?"

"Maybe, maybe not. I'm hoping he's just screening his calls, and when he sees it's you, he'll want to talk."

"Whatever man. I've been calling him, and he hasn't picked up yet. Anything, in particular, you want me to say?"

Brad was still annoyed over the way the conversation had been going.

"Just say what comes naturally, don't mention my being here and see if you can either find out where he is or get him to come over here for some reason."

"Yeah, I don't think he's coming here. He's far out of the way, and his wife keeps him on a short leash during the weekend."

Brad picked up his phone and spoke Larry's name. While the phone dialed Larry's number, he started to put it on speaker, but Wilkes shook his head no. After several rings, it went over to voicemail. Brad left a brief message asking Larry if he was doing alright and to call him when he could.

"Good enough." Wilkes sighed. "Let's see if he calls you back in a few minutes. While we're waiting, do you remember anything else from last night? Like the gun?"

Shaking his head, Brad said, "Not a gun! It's like I told you last night. It looked like a rock. Black, umm...polished and almost glowing. But in the dark and with all the rain, I couldn't tell exactly what I was seeing. I couldn't tell if it was glowing or a reflection from the streetlight bouncing off the rain."

"Yeah, that's what you said last night. Your buddy actually saw the weapon discharge. But other than that, your stories were the same. The girl had nothing on that, but she got a better look at the muggers."

Brad raised his eyebrows at that and looked directly at the sketch lying on the coffee table.

Wilkes just shook his head and picked up the sketch, folding it and put it into his pocket.

"I need a while to decide how I feel about what you said before I ask anybody else to look at this," said Wilkes as his phone rang. He answered quickly.

"Wilkes! Yeah, I'm still here. No. What?" he glanced at Brad as he stood up and started putting on his jacket. Wilkes paused as he listened to what was obviously his partner on the other end. "I'll be right there. Are the ME and crime scene guys there yet? Anyone else? We won't be on this much longer, so we better get our shit together now...What? When? Are you kidding me? So, help me, Fish, if you... okay, okay. Well, that'll do it for sure. The Feds will be all over this now. Be there in 30."

He swiped end and dropped the phone in his pocket.

"What was that all about? What's going on?" Brad asked in rapid succession.

Making eye contact with Brad, Wilkes gave him a head-tilting look.

"Why are you so jumpy?"

"Well, my partner's at Ellsworth's house. He's not there. But his wife is...She's dead."

Brad paused, trying to think of what to say. All he could manage was, "What?"

Wilkes observed Brad's reaction and decided it was a real shock. That was mildly reassuring. "Dead! No cars at the house, and no signs of him. So, your pal's on the run. We now have a kidnapping in Seattle and in California. The FBI is going to be all over this case. Yesterday, a couple of people in Hawaii claimed that some larger-than-life figures

58

attacked them. And that these assailants took two other people." What he didn't tell Brad was that the Hawaiians had told the investigating officers that the kidnappers looked like Tiki carvings.

"Are you headed to Larry's? I'm coming with you," Brad said as he got up and went to grab a coat.

Wilkes, wanting to follow procedure said, "No, you can't, but what can you do is let me know if Ellsworth calls you. And whatever you do, do not let him know that you know what we've found at his house."

Brad stood at his entry coat closet with the door open, "Come on, Wilkes, after what happened last night, don't I deserve this? I mean, these are my friends. Look at what's going on here. What am I supposed to do, just sit on my ass?"

"That's exactly what I want you to do. Listen, you aren't a cop, so you wouldn't know that I've already brought you more into the loop than I should have. But if I bring you along at this stage, it will cause no problems for both of us. So, stay here or stick to your usual Saturday routine, and I'll be in touch. I'll let you know if we find Ellsworth. Were you close with his wife?"

Brad shrugged.

"No. I don't know anybody that was close to Natalie."

"They have problems? Did she cheat?"

Brad appeared to be carefully pondering his response.

"Yes, they had problems but not...violent. At least, not that I knew of. I don't know if Natalie cheated, but they were always arguing about something. Maybe...wait, you said 'dead.' You think it was murder?"

"Hell yeah I think it was murder. Look, I've got to go. I'll keep you informed as much as I can."

Brad gritted his teeth, shut the closet door, and rubbed the back of his neck.

"Right. Fine."

Opening the front door and stepping over the threshold, Wilkes turned and looked back at Brad as he walked out and pulled the door behind him. Something wasn't right here, and he was damn sure going to figure out what it was.

"Stay out of my way," Wilkes said as he closed the door and walked down the hallway.

Chapter Nine:

Unknown Location

Jack and Daniel took several steps back and nervously got closer to each other. The door was slowly receding into the wall. As it retreated more into the wall, a short hallway appeared. Jack and Daniel glanced quickly at each other, then Jack looked back at Maddy, who had moved behind the couch she was sitting on. The retreating door stopped and slowly slid sideways.

A tall figure stepped into the hallway and began walking purposefully toward them. They took an involuntary step back. As the silhouetted figure approached, Jack could see that it was human in shape but very tall. Not the body or image of the strange giants he had encountered before but more of a normal human form. As it got closer, fine details became more pronounced: Male, clothed in loose nondescript garments that fell to calf length, and belted at the waist. The arms and legs were bare. Long hair brushed broad, muscular shoulders. Emerging into the room's light, the man stopped and silently surveyed the surroundings.

He had to be almost eight feet tall. And while he appeared human, his features were too perfect and seemingly off. His head was crowned with a mane that was a polished gold color, not blond, but gold, and seemed to be made of metal strands rather than human hair. His clothing was gray, and the belt cinched at his waist was a rope of what looked like woven silver. His features resembled those of sculptures from the Renaissance period. His skin was smooth, with no visible pores, like a child or a living sculpture carved from marble. It gave him an artificial appearance, although the color of his skin was a golden brown and had a healthy glow. No hair or blemish marred any of his limbs. His face was handsome, but his eyes were bizarre to the extreme. Large and almond-shaped, they were an almost iridescent blue. All blue. No white, no iris to speak of, and no pupil. Unless the gold and silver flecks amidst the blue were multiple pupils. Were they some kind of artificial lens? Jack had seen some characters on the streets of downtown Seattle, wearing contact lenses with every type of weird design imaginable. But these were different from anything he had ever seen.

Strolling through the room, he went first to the unconscious forms of the woman and the two men. Kneeling by each one, he placed his hand over their hearts, and after seeming to assure himself that they were unharmed, he turned back to Jack and Daniel.

"You are in no danger from me. You will not be harmed." His voice was so deep and robust.

Daniel and Jack walked to the couch where Maddy stood after looking at each other for guidance and support. Maddy was so nervous that her hands went white from clenching the back of the sofa so hard. Daniel and Jack sat down on the couch first, then Maddy slowly walked around the side and sat beside Jack. Jack thought the situation was almost comical. It was like three children being confronted by their parent. Albeit an otherworldly parent.

The tall pseudo human moved to a position directly facing the three.

"You will stay here for a short time, and then you will be released. You will retain your memories of all that has transpired but be warned: should you attempt to profit from your experiences or engage in any behavior that could prove harmful to our commitment, you may be lost."

Just what in the hell is this guy talking about, Jack wondered. Released? Where are we anyway? In another country, in a warehouse, or on a crazy aircraft? Profit? But perhaps most disturbing of all was the subtle threat 'you may be lost'. What does that mean?

"Can we ask you why these things have happened to us?" said Jack.

Encouraged by Jack's question, Maddy leaned forward and said, "Yeah, why are we here? Who are you? What are you? What is this place? When do we go home? What gives you the right to take us from our lives?"

Daniel snorted, "That kinda covers all my questions. At least for the moment."

The pseudo human's large, strange eyes, with gold flecks flashing and shifting, passed over each of the three and rested on Daniel.

"Disrespectful? No. Fear." He walked over to an oversized chair and moved it to face the couch.

Looking over his shoulder, Jack saw that the others were still unconscious.

"What about them?" he asked. "Why are they still out? Shouldn't they hear this? Are they hurt?"

Seating himself facing the three, the tall, stranger began speaking softly in an even, well-modulated voice.

"Questions. Limited ways in which to respond while protecting our Captain's intent. That by which I am called is of no importance. But for your simple dialogue, you may refer to me as Healer. My presence is purposed to assure your well-being and good health. The others remain sleeping for unique reasons." He said as he waved his hand to indicate the unconscious figures.

"The young man brought from the island is still healing. He has suffered many injuries." Jack thought he saw mild disapproval in Healer's glance at Daniel.

"The woman was brought here in error." With another casual wave of his golden hand, the black woman disappeared. No sparks, no fanfare, no special effects. Just there and then not there. Maddy took a deep breath but remained silent. Jack clenched his fists, bracing himself for whatever might come next. Daniel just glanced at the Healer and whistled softly.

"And him," he indicated the body sprawled in the far corner, "is being cleansed. He will wake soon. The right or authority to bring you here comes from our Captain, and that is all the 'RIGHT' we require. Your ways, and laws are not ours. This," a grand sweeping gesture indicating their surroundings, "is a structure that exists only to accommodate you. When you leave this place, all you see here will cease to be. You are here for your protection and to be prepared. When you are made ready, you will leave." A faint smile played about the too-perfect lips.

Jack's mind was spinning. They had been abducted by aliens who will program them for some nefarious scheme and then turn them loose to serve their will.

Healer? Is that a name or a vocation?

Jack dug his fingernails into his palms until they almost drew blood, trying to get his mind focused. This entire scenario was utterly off the nuts. Maddy was aggressive in her attitude, and Daniel didn't seem fazed by what was happening. Was that another symptom of shock? Or had he figured something out that had escaped Jack's notice? Jack was glad he was already seated because he felt woozy and nauseous. Every moment brought more fantastically unbelievable information. The Healer spoke of a 'Captain' and others: 'Your ways and laws are not ours.' Where was the rest of his alien crew? And he had said they were being protected. From what? The only thing Jack figured they needed saving from was the gray-faced goons that had abducted them all. What else had he said? Prepared? Prepared how and for what? Every answer just created more questions.

As if reading Jack's mind, Healer spoke.

"I can anticipate your next questions. I will not answer all of them. You cannot know at this time all that you desire to know. But the most vital fact you should know is that you are important, and each has a special and unique place in the order of things that must be."

"Whoops, ending a sentence in a preposition. How gauche! Aliens today, you just can't teach 'em grammar." Daniel joked. The others looked at him with incredulous stares.

"What? This is all so heavy. We need a little banter."

Turning to get a good look at Daniel, Jack said, "actually, be is an irregular verb not a preposition. And by the way, where'd your Hawaiian accent and broken English get off to?"

Daniel smiled and spread his hands out in front of him, "I mostly talk that way when I'm with my friends. Twelve years with Franciscan nuns and living with a loving grandmother, what can I say? My French teacher would be proud of me. Gauche is French, you know. My best subject in school. I love the romance languages."

Healer rose smoothly and gracefully from his chair. His head was slightly inclined as he gazed down at Daniel.

Jumping up from the couch, Maddy looked angrily at Daniel.

"What are you doing? Jokes? Seriously?" She turned to Healer, eyes flashing, her voice rising angrily, "If we're to be protected, then I want to leave right now! Take me home. I don't want to be 'prepared,' and you can just count me out if we aren't to be harmed. I mean right now!"

With sympathetic tones and a demeanor that bespoke sadness, Healer spoke, "That, child of earth, I cannot do. Your role, your part, however small, is part of a design that is beyond your wants and control."

Maddy's chest was heaving, and a sweat had broken out on her upper lip.

"You big, weird piece of shit! You stole us from our home, hell right off the street and brought us here against our will. You said we wouldn't be harmed...well, being here is harming ME! You're 'purposed' with making sure we're okay? Well, I'm not okay! I'll be okay when you send me back. However, you do that," she waved her hands in the air, "and then I can wake up and pretend this was all just a fucking nightmare!"

Taking one long step toward the couch, Healer stood before Maddy and reached out to touch her shoulder. Initially, she jerked away from his touch, but on his second attempt, when his hand made contact, all the tension in her melted. She relaxed, and her breathing slowed.

"You misunderstand me. The choice to return you is not my decision, nor is it yours." He stood back and removed his hand. Much calmer but unwilling to let it go, Maddy continued in a more level tone of voice.

"What if we just followed you down that hall? What if we asked your Captain? What if we fought you? How would that work, seeing as you are responsible for us?"

Healer looked blankly at Maddy.

"What has befallen you is strange. You are confused. You may ultimately render yourself useless as originally intended, but you will still serve. You will not be allowed to follow me. You will not interact with any hosts until we decide you are ready to do so. And I will not allow you to injure yourselves by attempting to engage me physically. Can you not see? I need not raise my hand against you to restrain you. Be at peace. Be calm. I will not continue this discussion if it creates anxiety within you." Healer turned and was about to leave.

Jack got to his feet. "Wait!"

Healer stopped and turned his swirling gaze on Jack.

Feeling as though an opportunity to make sense of their situation was literally walking out the door, Jack asked, "Who are you? What are you? How are we going to be prepared? Those things that brought us here, what were they? And...and...and how do you speak English?"

"We have been watching you and all humans for millennia. We are not, as you can certainly see, human. The preparation you are so curious and concerned about will be clear if my Captain decides to speak to you. It is his choice, not mine. The creatures who obtained you are seeking a kind of redemption. I speak English to you because that is your all of your native tongues; you would not understand me were I to address you in the language of my kind, Kliflojasy. I am sorry that the designation Healer seems not to satisfy."

With that, he turned again, walked to the doorway, and into the hall beyond. Maddy took a few tentative steps after him as though to follow and then stopped.

"Are we just going to let him go?" She pleaded with Jack.

Watching the retreating figure, Jack turned to face her, feeling helpless.

"Do you really think we could stop him if we tried?"

Laughing, Daniel offered, "Oh, sure. You betcha. That'd last like maybe two seconds. That's some serious magic or, I don't know what, but there's something powerful going on all around that dude."

Jack looked down at his hands, where his fingernails had indented small crescents into his palm.

"Well, I guess we can officially say that we're fucked. And not in a good way."

Chapter Ten:

Seattle, Washington

A steady rain pelted the street in a passionless rhythm. The pale drops tore dying leaves from the trees lining the street, as if jealous of their color. Cars raced along the street, their tires making a sizzling sound on the slick asphalt. The windshield wipers of Larry's car worked silently and efficiently to provide a clear view of the road ahead. At least he could enjoy Nat's Lexus while he was figuring his way out of the mess he was in.

Enjoy? Well, that is a stretch, but he could appreciate it. Quiet. Smooth. Safe.

Larry needed those things because he had some serious thinking to do. His phone had been going off non-stop for hours. The business calls were bad enough but could be dealt with later. The alerts bugging him were the constant barrage from the SPD and now Brad. He didn't know if he could trust Brad. He also worried that he couldn't tell if the cops were with him.

At least the calls from the SPD had stopped for a while. Why was that? He wondered if they had tried to reach him at home, and if so, had they managed to track down his actual address? Possibly. He wasn't unlisted, but he'd given some phony information when they questioned him. He hadn't wanted them showing up in the middle of the night.

The red Lexus cut through the rain and pulled up to Brad's condominium building. It was the most luxurious and impressive building in an area known for its wealthy residents. Larry sat and reviewed his planned approach to Brad. Had he picked the best way to tell him? How would he react? Changing his mind about parking on the street, he got into traffic again and executed a U-turn. He doubled back and drove into the building's parking garage. He selected a space far from the entrance and the elevator. He parked the car, not necessarily hidden from view, so the Lexus wouldn't be immediately spotted if someone were just driving by. They would have to enter the garage and specifically look for it.

Larry leaned back in the seat and closed his eyes. Things had been moving too fast the last thirty-six hours, and he hadn't slept. He was having trouble concentrating, and just needed a minute or two to relax. Gripping the steering wheel, he closed his eyes and tried to clear his mind. He did some simple breathing exercises to slow his heart rate and forced himself to relax. Exiting the car, he stood up, stretched, and closed the door behind him.

Putting all the negative thoughts out of his mind, he moved quickly to the elevator. It was time to put things to the test. He needed to talk with Brad before he could plan his next move.

If things went sideways, he would just have to deal with it.

Chapter Eleven:

West Seattle, Washington

The rain came down in sheets and flooded the windshield of the Crown Victoria. The wipers labored to provide any visibility at all. The first sounds of distant thunder rumbled like some ancient call to arms.

Flexing his hands, Wilkes shifted his grip on the steering wheel, fighting the numbness that crept in on long rides. He grunted irritably as he shifted his weight in the seat. He stared out through the windshield, watching the pattern of the raindrops streak across the flooded glass. The years were catching up to him, he thought. He was still tough enough to hold his own with the young guys, but he would spend hours at the end of the day thinking about retirement.

He was saddled with a new partner who had too much nervous energy and asked the same questions he'd heard for decades with the SPD. It had been even more difficult lately. Wilkes and Fisher had been pulled off one of the most prominent cases in Seattle. The missing women. The women and their abductors were now in the purview of the FBI and an elite task force that didn't include detectives nearing retirement. Fisher and Wilkes had some negative interactions with the Chief of Detectives, and being pulled from the case was a quasi-retaliation.

Shifting his grip again, he glanced at the old gnarled hands that seemed to belong to someone else. How did I get so old so fast? Well, is fifty really that old? He thought to himself.

His hands hurt more when the weather was wet and cold, making him feel older than he was.

He fumbled the lid off the foam cup and tossed it onto the dash with several others. The heat from the coffee felt good in his hand. He brought the coffee to his lips when his cell phone vibrated against his waist. As he placed the cup onto the center console to answer the phone, it spilled on the seat and his hand. Ripping the phone from the leather holder, he angrily swiped answer.

"Wilkes!" he snapped without looking at the caller ID.

"Whoa, is that any way to talk to a brother?" said a familiar voice.

Sighing and relaxing as he recognized his ex-partner's voice, Wilkes replied,

"What's up, Mitch?"

"Just reaching out regarding your grab and the B&E down here you were so curious about. Anything new on your end?"

"New? Yeah, there's a whole lot of shit going on here."

While deciding not to relate every detail of his conversation with Brad Mayo, Wilkes brought his old partner up to speed on the general developments of the case, including the story coming out of Hawaii.

Letting his breath out slowly, Mitch asked,

"Who do you like for the murder? The husband?"

"Oh, yeah. He's a piece of work. Played games during the interview last night and then pulled a fast one with his address. It looks like the killer used a knife. Real nasty business. Definitely seems to be personal. We're trying to run him down now, and since he's probably driving the wife's red Lexus, we got that working for us."

"A red Lexus. Man, he's got some balls driving around in a neon sign. Balls or just plain stupid. BOLO working?"

"Yep. Should hear something any time. Have you heard anything new about the smash and snatch in Century City? Any other witnesses come forward?"

"Nah, but I hear that the whole thing isn't gonna be on the local plate much longer. The Feds will throw the B&E with potential kidnap into a package and call it theirs."

"Yeah, love the FBI. I'm going to be seeing them here soon, then. But the murder will be my leverage for staying in the case." Wilkes grunted.

"Careful partner. Stick your foot in a federal crack, and they just might break it off."

"Funny. Like, that's the first time I've heard that one. Have you been savin' that all day?"

"All damn day my friend." Mitch chuckled with more than a tinge of sarcasm.

"Look, Dave, I can keep feeding you stuff on this problem in Century City, but it isn't my deal. Sooner or later, the information stream will dry up. Capeesh?"

"Yeah, yeah. I know. It could be nothing but the descriptions and the timing; it all screams coincidence. And you know what we say about that."

"Uh-huh. No such thing."

"Right."

"Yeah, well, be safe. It's pouring here. I'm trying not to kill myself on this drive. Call me if you get anything new." He tapped end on the screen.

The conversation suddenly reminded Wilkes of another matter he wanted to resolve quickly. He needed to visit the scene at the Ellsworth residence, but he also remembered his idea for a second interview with Cheyenne Johnson, the young lady who had been left behind with Mayo and Ellsworth. He was going to need some help. He tapped his screen and voice dialed his favorite 'go-to' person at police headquarters.

A smoky feminine voice answered, "SPD Records, Bernice here. How can I help you?"

Bernice Watkins had worked for the Seattle Police Department for over thirty years. Years ago, she had been transferred to Records over on Stacy Street. The SPD was her entire life. She had become a valued resource for Wilkes. Whenever he needed some help with one detail or another, Bernice was all over it, as long as she got a little inside information on what was going down.

"Bernice, baby, what's new?" Wilkes asked.

"Baby? Don't baby me, Dave Wilkes. I know your voice, and I know your act. What do you need?" The voice on the phone snorted.

"Bernice, I'm hurt. You sayin' we ain't pals?"

"Stop, Dave. It's been really busy here all day, and I'm already into double-digit OT this week. What do you need?"

"At least you're getting the OT. I need a prop for an interview I will schedule later today." Wilkes Chuckled.

Always to the point, Bernice would press for some juicy details at another time when it was convenient for her.

"I'm sure. What is it? When do you need it?" She asked.

Wilkes filled her in on what he was looking for, when he needed it, and where. Bernice let him know she would take care of it, and that was the gospel as far as Wilkes was concerned.

Picking up his coffee, he took a sip and felt it warm him. Cold rain, a storm rolling in, and a hot cup of coffee. A little bit of relaxation in the middle of what was already turning out to be a terrible day. And a busy one.

His mind naturally drifted back to the details of the case. He couldn't figure out the Ellsworth woman's death in all this. Did that happen after the mugging? Was the mugging a setup Ellsworth had arranged to create an alibi and control the narrative? The other pieces just didn't fit. The Century City burglary with a possible kidnapping was one thing, but the descriptions given by the beach bums in Hawaii put everything in a new light. No way all these stories could be fabricated. Plus, they were so geographically far apart and within just two days of each other. If he could put it together, it was a safe bet that the feds could too. Nothing had leaked to the internet yet, so there couldn't be any pollution from the information cesspool. The internet was a curse when it came to working on a case that attracted significant media interest.

So, there were attacks in three separate locations. All three involved kidnappings or a suspected kidnapping since the kid in So Cal wasn't officially missing yet. Different sex and ethnic variables. They are too far apart to be the same perps. No connection between the victims or intended victims. Witnesses coming up with similar identifications, despite Mayo's off-the-wall comment. No physical evidence was left at the scene except for Ellsworth's damaged shirt. Ellsworth was the wild card in the deck. His behavior in the interview, the fake personal information, and subsequent disappearance all pointed to another agenda. Could it just be that a murderer had the bad luck to be a victim of another crime and got brought in by happenstance? There are no coincidences, Wilkes told himself, and he would bet that the ME would return with a time of death well before the alley mugging.

Wilkes sighed and took another swig of coffee. Getting too cold to be good.

He liked his coffee hot. The way Betty had always had it waiting for him in the morning before he left for work.

BETTY.

The thought of her wrenched another sigh from him. Two years had passed, and it still hurts whenever he thinks of her. Her sweet smile. Her light touch on his shoulder. He missed it all, but mostly he missed knowing she would be there at the end of the day.

NO MORE.

Gone on to her reward, like she always said when someone passed away. And for her, he hoped that was true. No one deserves it more.

'You're so loyal and strong. When you finally answer the call, you'll be a fierce warrior for Christ.' She had been fond of saying.

His smart-ass response had typically been something along the lines of, 'Call? What call? I'm right here, and I don't hear anything.' She would invariably respond with, 'He's calling you every day, and when you're finally ready, you'll find out that he's been waiting on you all along.'

The job had helped him stay grounded during the early months, but the empty house waiting for him caused him to often just put in more time. His daughter was all grownup and raising her own family. Still, the infrequent calls had begun to come even less frequently to the point where they were uncomfortable when they did talk. And he felt like shit afterward.

Mad at himself for not being better at relationships and deeply saddened that the best thing he and Betty had made together was slowly pulling away. Betty had always been the one to keep all the connections fresh. Keep up with family, send cards, and remember birthdays. He'd never been good at that, and her gift for that kind of thing had made it easy to take it for granted. Now he heard from the family once or twice a year.

Best to just throw himself into the case and do what he did best.

Squaring his shoulders, changing his grip, and shifting his weight, he sat up straight behind the wheel and increased his speed as though reaching his destination faster would relieve his pain.

Thirty minutes later, the Crown Vic pulled into a classy suburban neighborhood. Lush, well-tended yards in front of luxurious, custom homes set on large lots. The Ellsworth home was a three-story house, painted slate grey with light grey trim. From a distance, it practically blended with the stormy sky.

Several news vans were crowded into the cul-de-sac. Wilkes parked out front next to Fisher's SUV. An ME van and several other cars that probably belonged to CSI were parked along the long driveway. Yellow crime scene tape had been wrapped around landscaping and a mailbox to barricade the entrance to the property. Reporters, some with camera crews trailing them, turned in his direction. Without making eye contact and ignoring their shouted questions, he ducked under the tape and headed for the entrance in the steady rain. A uniformed officer in rain gear nodded to him as he walked by and climbed the large cobblestone walkway.

The front door was open, and Fisher stood just inside waiting for him. He was ashen-faced and looked on the verge of being ill.

Nodding at Fisher, Wilkes asked, "How's the Hot Dog business?" Fisher owned a Hot Dog shack down on the waterfront. He had hoped that the business would help subsidize his civil servant pay.

"Not good. And don't talk about food, for crying out loud."

"We got a TOD yet? Who's in from CSI? Break it down for me." Wilkes rasped as he looked at his partner's shaky appearance.

Nodding and pointing upstairs, Fisher responded, "Yeah, yeah. Between one and four pm yesterday. The CSI detective is some tiny chick. Don't know her."

"Any surprises when they gave you the cause? You said he used a knife when we talked earlier."

Wilkes started heading up the stairs, grumbling to himself about the new CSI detective. He hoped she wasn't a pain in the ass. As he reached the second-floor landing, he could hear several people working and caught the first whiff of a strong, unmistakable odor.

Following behind him, Fisher cleared his throat, "No knife. An Axe or hatchet maybe. But that wasn't the murder weapon. Blow to the head, but there's other stuff too. It's a real horror show in there, man." His body language indicated he was uncomfortable explaining any specifics about the cause of death, which was unlike him. Having been a homicide detective for nine years, Fisher had seen enough not to be easily rattled.

Wilkes raised an eyebrow attempting to draw him out, but Fisher just shook his head and stood back as they approached the master bedroom. The smell was now almost overpowering. Glancing back at Fisher, Wilkes wondered what was spooking him.

He entered the bedroom and suddenly didn't wonder anymore.

Mrs. Ellsworth murdered in rather spectacular fashion.

Four members of the CSI unit and the medical examiner's office were working the room, taking photographs, dusting for prints, and using numerous evidence markers throughout the room to tag the grisly remains of Natalie Ellsworth. Bloody stains and pieces of her everywhere. Taking a shallow breath and trying to close his nostrils, Wilkes looked around the room and recognized Martin Phipps, an ME he'd worked with many times.

"Geez, Martin. What the hell?" He indicated the contents of the room with a glance.

Without looking up, the slender, bespectacled examiner responded with an exasperated tone, "Yeah. This is all I need after three 14-hour days working a shootout."

Hesitating a few seconds, Wilkes carefully agreed.

"Yeah. Fisher says you have time and cause. Talk to me." Wilkes placed his feet carefully to avoid disturbing the cluttered crime scene.

Turning slowly to take in the room, Phipps shrugged, "Mmhmm...yes, early afternoon yesterday between one and four, give or take. The temp and rigor readings are off because of the dismemberment, which obviously took place several hours after death. The lividity makes it a little easier, but that was interrupted by the cutting, so...," noticing Wilkes's expression of frustration, he hurried to finish, "...anyway cause of death was likely a blow to the head."

"No knife? Fisher said it was an axe. And all this..."

"Occurred after the killing blow," Phipps said as he looked up owlishly.

"Okay. Good." Wilkes blew out a breath and tried to adjust to the smell that enveloped the bedroom.

Phipps paused a second to address one of his assistants, "Stop! I want each piece bagged separately. For God's sake! Have you ever worked a crime scene before?"

Turning back to Wilkes, Phipps said, "Okay then, I'll see you later and have a more detailed assessment ready for you." He turned and resumed packing a cooler and his medical kit, clearly considering the discussion with Wilkes over.

Wilkes could feel someone standing behind him and turned to find a member of the CSI unit waiting to get his attention. She was slender, a little on the mousey side, with a pinched look around the face. Or maybe that was just the result of the heavy odor in the death room. She tilted her head up and waited for Wilkes to start the conversation.

"You the lead?"

"Detective Wilkes?" She nodded.

"Yes. You met my partner, Detective Fisher. What have you got?"

Gloved hands at her side, one holding a Rofin Polilight, she said,

"Wren Jenkins. A new detective was assigned to SPD CSI. We agree with the ME's assessment. Virtually no splatter, no defensive marks, and some blood traces on the bed where she most likely died. Head trauma and blood around the wound indicate that's probably where the killing blow landed. Most of the cutting occurred on the floor next to the bed, with all that occurring post-mortem. Plenty of prints, but none marked with blood traces, so we'll have to sort that out later. No weapon yet. We have someone checking the other rooms, perimeter, and trash cans. Computer forensics puts someone else, probably the husband, in the house around the time of death. Home-based business and lots of computer access before the TOD window. Vic's laptop showed lots of activity almost right up to the TOD. No activity during or after the dismemberment on the desktop downstairs but some

81

activity on the laptop afterward. There was no blood trail from the bedroom, so the cleanup occurred there."

She clicked the Polilight on and off, indicating they had scanned for DNA traces with it. "Nothing in the trash in the master bath. Pretty clinical."

Wilkes was impressed. "What do you make of the time between death and...all the activity afterward?"

Shaking her head, she said, "I'm not sure. All the pieces are here, so a positive ID isn't going to be a problem. So, masking the victim's identity wasn't the goal; maybe an attempt to obscure the time of death. That didn't work, though. Nothing ritualistic, no note or articles placed with the body...parts. Seems pretty clear it was the husband. It's hard to say what he was trying to achieve. The activity on the laptop is kind of creepy."

"Creepy? Porn?"

"No. The internet searches had been deleted, as well as the history. Didn't matter. Forensics recovered all of it. Weird."

Wilkes was irritated with her beating around the bush.

"Yeah? Well, what was it?"

"Hundreds of pages all centered around the Emerald City Vanishings. Blogs, news pages, video journals, everything you could think of with disappearances. Creepy when you consider that she was obviously obsessed with it right up to the end and look at what happened to her." Jenkins waved the Polilight casually around the room without following the motion with her eyes.

"Plus, what's the motivation for doing a sloppy job of deleting pages and then leaving the laptop behind?

Whoever did it must have been some kind of idiot. If you know enough to remove the stuff, you should know enough to realize it's all still on there. Her car is gone. We went over the garage earlier, and there was no blood evidence on the first pass. Also seems clear that there was a lot of care taken in cleaning up. None of the details add up. The careful planning and violence after the fact indicate premeditation, but why leave her behind at that point? Completely disconnected. I think he may have experienced a psychotic break. We've got an unpredictable individual here. No apparent progression and no history of aberrant behavior. It's like a cork popping out of a champagne bottle. Who knows how long this mess has been brewing inside this guy. I'm betting he'll kill somebody else. It could be soon. Probably the first person to disappoint him or get in his way."

Wilkes' mind started working. Where would Ellsworth have to go? Who would he turn to? And what in the hell did the stuff with the laptop mean? There aren't enough hours in the day, he thought to himself. He needed to follow up on what little he had, but he also needed some sleep. He hadn't slept well the night before. He knew that lack of sleep would dull his senses and weaken his ability to work the case properly. While they were all sleeping, what would Ellsworth be doing? A feeling of dread crept over Wilkes.

Chapter Twelve:

Unknown Place

Opening his eyes, Jack awoke feeling rested and clear-headed. He knew exactly where he was. He looked around the room noting that all the others were still asleep. Jack laid there reviewing the last two day's events. Unbelievable. This was the kind of stuff that, were you to tell anyone about it, would get you classified as a lunatic. He started to wonder how many of those people had seen what they claimed. His estimate as of today was definitely higher than it would have been, say, three days ago.

Whether it had been due to all the excitement, unanswered questions weighing on their minds, physical fatigue, or perhaps some trickery on the part of their hosts, they'd been fighting to stay awake. They had reluctantly agreed to get some sleep amongst each other. Carefully, they moved the unconscious man to the couches so that he would be more comfortable. While they were moving the tanned surfer, Daniel was perplexed by the lack of visible injuries. He, at some point, confessed to Jack and Maddy that the young man was so badly beaten that Daniel feared he was going to die. Thankful that the young man was apparently in good shape but embarrassed and confused, Daniel had gone on to describe his troublesome friendship with Kimmo and Takele. He also spoke to his recent resolution to cut ties with them. That led to Daniel revealing more of his background, including that he lived with, and had been raised by, his grandmother, which struck a chord with Jack.

Maddy decided to share as well. She had grown up in a relatively average and typical middle-class family. After graduating from Stanford University in California, she and some friends took the summer off to do some traveling. She was trying to find a job in her field, but was having trouble. It was only recently that she started working at 13 Coins to pay the bills. She had moved back in with her parents and knew they would be looking for her. She was worried that her disappearance would devastate them. Concerned for her parents and little sister, Maddy had shed a few tears. Her spirited nature, sincere vulnerability, and beauty strongly affected Jack. He reached out to touch her shoulder for comfort and support. She placed her hand over his and thanked him. His skin seemed to tingle where she placed her hand. Trying to catch his breath Jack mumbled, "Confucius says, 'Our greatest glory is not in never falling, but in rising every time we fall', so we have to keep going, okay?"

"Okay", Maddy says with a slight smile.

The conversation had inevitably moved to their present predicament. Collectively, they had attempted to piece together an idea of what was happening. The fifth group member was still a mystery to them all. Jack and Maddy were taken together, as had Daniel and the other surfer. But the other young man, he was taken alone. Healer had indicated he was being 'cleansed,' which they had surmised meant detoxification from drugs or alcohol. Just how that was being accomplished, was a mystery to them.

Discussing their respective encounters with the Nephilim, they exchanged details of their confrontations. They agreed that Daniel's experience had yielded the most information. He had seen more of the giants' features and attributes; like Healer, they had spoken perfect English. Their almost brutish appearance starkly contrasted with Healer's, but what that might represent was frustratingly unclear. Different races indeed, and they also seemed to be some vague caste system based on how Healer referred to them. The rock-like weapon had been discussed at length, including the fact that while incredibly effective at stopping humans, it apparently didn't cause any lasting injury. Well, except maybe to polyester and cotton.

The eerie vanishing of the black woman had flustered them all. But it had revealed that Healer and his Capitan could make mistakes. Small comfort there, Jack thought. *We were abducted by mighty, mysterious beings who don't know exactly what they're doing. This is like some script from a comedy-horror film.*

Healer also said one of the reasons they had been taken was for their protection. Protected from what? Was there some upcoming event or conflict in which they were somehow involved? Winston Churchill's famous appraisal of Russian culture, 'A mystery, wrapped in a riddle, inside an enigma,' seemed ideally suited to describe their situation. And while Jack felt confident that they were likely to meet another member of Healer's race, potentially gaining more insight into their circumstances, he wondered what they might actually learn and how that would change things.

There were times when it seemed that an answer to a mystery might be right around the corner, and instead, there was something unexpected waiting for them.

While growing up on his uncle's ranch, Jack had been fascinated with the mystery of 'hog season.' Not that there was anything terribly difficult to understand. He knew they lived on a ranch and that animals were food, and there were lots of 'post-season' details that should have made the whole thing easy to figure out. The first day of the season started with lots of live full-grown hogs and ended with tons of fresh meat. Not a hog left in sight. The mere fact that he was not allowed to help or tag along because he was too young made the whole process mysterious, and an obsession for a small boy. That was until he was finally allowed to go with his older cousins after he turned eight years old. Just being in the company of his big cousin Mick was reason enough to be happy and excited. Mick was thirteen and practically a full-grown man. The adventure had started out innocently enough. There were the usual cautionary bits of advice and sharp commands to watch this and be careful of that. Jack hadn't minded that at all. Uncle John picked Jack up and placed him on the metal fencing, where he would have a perfect view of the hog run.

Jack was confused, "Why am I up here, Uncle John? Don't you want me on the ground to help you and Mick?"

"You can help out later little guy." Uncle John said.

"Don't worry, there will be plenty for you to do soon enough," said his other cousin Mark.

While Jack had settled onto his perch, Mark, Mick, and Uncle John had herded a giant hog into the run. To Jack, it looked as big as a car. A heavy metal gate swung behind the hog allowing no room for it to back up or move forward. The hog had raised its head, snout snorting, ears flicking, and beady eyes vainly seeking an exit. Without warning, Mark had appeared with a low-caliber rifle, placed it against the hog's head, and pulled the trigger. The hog had bucked and jerked. A spurt of hot blood from the mortally wounded animal had splashed on Jack. Surprised and disgusted, Jack fell backward into the dirt. Mark laughed as Uncle John ran around and pulled Jack to his feet.

"You okay, Jackie?"

"Yeah, I'm okay," Jack said with low annoyed tone. He hated that familial version of his name. It was a girl's name, and he didn't want Mick to think he was a girl. So, walked numbly back to the fence to watch the rest of the backbreaking work. It was small consolation that Uncle John had been trying to keep him out of the way and that the gory mess had resulted from Mark's poorly aimed shot. Showering later, he had fought back the tears and filed away the lesson.

Some questions have answers you might be happier not knowing.

Thinking about his family made Jack wistful. His Uncle John and Aunt Rose had long since passed away. Mick had moved to the Gulf Coast, and contact had become sporadic. Mark had engaged in a series of crimes that had finally landed him in jail, and Jack had no idea where he was now. With virtually no family left, he felt anonymous and alone.

Although Jack thought his clients were likely to miss him, would they be concerned enough to report him missing? The client expecting a completed web design would be especially interested in where Jack was, and why her design still needed to be completed. Jack almost laughed, thinking about how that conversation would sound. 'Yeah, so here's the thing...your project isn't done because I got kidnapped...by giants.' That would go over great! Good word-of-mouth advertising too!

Jack stifled a laugh and turned on his side, opening his eyes enough to allow another scan of the room. Daniel and Maddy had chosen couches of their own and appeared deep in sleep. Glancing over to the other men, he saw they were also sleeping.

He pushed his coat, serving as a too-small blanket, away and rubbed at his eyes. Sitting up and trying to be quiet, he stood and walked over to the mystery man. Jack couldn't quite place his ethnic background. His skin was white, but his features hinted at a Spanish heritage. A wispy mustache drooped over his mouth; his hair was a light brown, long and fine. His clothes were: ripped skinny jeans, faded black Vans, and a black T emblazoned with tribal tattoos and a familiar splash of white powder residue across the front. Like everyone else, he seemed unharmed and in good health, save for the bleached-out damage to his shirt. Looks like you had a run-in with the same bastards that shot me, he thought. Jack stretched out a hand and gave him a careful shake. Shifting slightly, he moved his hand up to scratch his jaw. Another nudge elicited a sigh, and his eyes opened. Mindful of Maddy's first response upon waking, Jack stepped back.

"Who the hell are you?" he said as he looked around. "And where the hell am I?"

Jack almost groaned out loud, "I've been answering those same questions repeatedly. My name's Jack Carpenter. You've been out for at least a day. And this place, what it is, and where it is are the questions that we all want an answer to. Ohh, and all of us were brought here by..."

"...huge butt ugly bastards that looked like Easter Island refugees?" The stranger finished.

Caught by surprise, Jack hesitated for a moment. Was that the vague image he had been trying to recall?

"Well, no. Maybe. I didn't look at them well, but that might...be right."

"My name's Rafael. Rafe. So, what's the deal here? Are we on a boat or something? What gives? I mean, are we like hostages or prisoners or what?"

"Well, that's not exactly clear right now. And the...thing that talked to us earlier was..."

"Not helpful. Okay, got it. Is there any food? I'm fucking starved!" Rafe asked as he looked around.

"We don't know exactly what's happening except that we were all taken and brought here. There's...no food...yet. Let me tell you what I know, and then I'd like to hear your story."

Rafe stood up and put his hands behind his back to stretch out.

"Sounds good. You're definitely not one of the guys who jumped me."

Looking across the room at Maddy and Daniel, he said, "Who're they?" Looking down at his chest, he saw the bleached damage.

"What? Oh, shit! What the hell is this?" Pulling up his shirt, he discovered no injury and looked at Jack.

Jack shook his head, "Better sit down, man; it'll take some time to fill you in."

"Maybe you can fill me in too. Just what in the world is going on around here?" said an unfamiliar voice. Turning to see who had spoken, the surfer had awoken and walked up behind them while they were talking.

Letting out a long breath, Jack said, "Well, at least I'll only have to say it once instead of repeating it for both of you."

They all sat, and Jack began describing the last two days' events.

Chapter Thirteen:

Seattle, Washington

Staring out the window, Brad watched the rain streak down the glass. It was really raining hard now. Hard enough to bend the trees. The rain and darkening skies had washed all the color out of the day, turning everything to shades of gray and blue.

He put his phone down and resisted the lure to call Larry again. The investigation into Natalie's death was weighing heavily on him. Brad had never been as close to Larry as he was to Jack. Larry had always been the oddball in the group when they were in college. Over the years, several people had expressed curiosity over his friendship with Larry. Brad had always laughed it off with the explanation that sometimes you didn't pick your friends; they chose you.

Turning away from the window, he got up and walked into his den to sit at his desk. Like everything in the condo, the desk and computer were state of the art. Integrated holographic touch screen embedded in the top of the desk, 500 terabyte hard drive, and all the top-end components. The computer, always on, flashed that he had several voicemails and flash emails waiting for him. Ordinarily, he would spend an hour or so responding to messages and surfing the net, but he wasn't feeling it at the moment. Leaning back in his chair, he could feel all the tension returning. Everything was spinning out of control. Irrevocably changed.

The detective had pushed him, but all things considered, it was probably harmless. For a cranky old fuck, that is. Brad shook his head, trying not to think about the shock of recognition he'd had when he looked at the police sketch. He wondered if Larry had gotten a good enough look at the muggers to validate his memory of their appearance. He needed to speak to Larry face to face. Walking back into his living room, Brad was headed into the kitchen to grab a beer when his phone rang. The personalized tone indicated it was a friend, and not a business associate. He hurried over to it and saw Larry's number and video clip playing on the screen. Hesitating only a minute, he picked up the phone and tapped the screen.

"Hello."

A pause on the other end was followed by someone clearing their throat.

"Brad? It's Larry. Are you alone?"

"Yeah, why? What's up?" Play it cool, Brad thought, don't spook him.

"I'm in trouble, man. I'm in your building, but I...need to know for sure that you're alone."

"Larry, quit screwing around and come on up. Are you out front or in the garage?"

"I'm in the elevator."

"Come on up. Today's code is 110778. Then hit pound."

"Okay, see you in a minute."

Brad had long ago given Jack, Larry, and one or two ladies, the code for entering the elevator, but Larry would still need to be buzzed through at the penthouse level.

Tapping the phone and ending the connection, Brad thought quickly. Should I call Wilkes? Or should I hear Larry out first? He decided he needed to be careful and play this correctly. Any lack of timely communication could land him right in the shit. He needed to play this right.

He walked back into the den and found the card Wilkes had given him the night before when they were released. Entering the number quickly, he opened the connection. The line rang once and rolled over to voicemail. He left a quick message for Wilkes and ended the call.

"Hey, it's Brad. Larry just called."

Hustling back out to the kitchen, he pulled a beer out of the fridge, opened it, and set it on the counter. He pulled a couple of magazines over to the counter to make it look like he was looking through them. His phone chimed. The screen identified Wilkes as the caller. He tapped the screen and started speaking immediately.

"Wilkes, I can't talk. He's in the building."

He hung up and had barely put the phone down when he heard a knock at the door.

Chapter Fourteen:

Seattle, Washington

Early commuter traffic had turned the I-5 corridor into its daily imitation of a parking lot. The storm just made it worse. Minutes dragged by with little to no progress. Wilkes was in no man's land on the bridge, where there was no opportunity to skirt the traffic jam by driving on the shoulder. Fuming from the frustration, he kept honking and flashing his lights at the cars in front of him to no avail. He'd been forced to call in a patrol unit from the adjacent precinct and ask for them to get to Mayo's because there was no possible way that he would make it in an hour. Wilkes felt that closing the murder should be a slam dunk, but they needed a weapon and blood evidence to lock it down. He worried that the patrolmen would screw it up somehow and taint the evidence trail. The last call had ended with him being angry enough to question their competence, which had aggravated the patrolmen. Perfect, he thought. Now it'll become a self-fulfilling prophecy.

He couldn't risk calling Mayo back for fear of tipping off Ellsworth. One unexplained or suspicious phone call could cause him to run or worse.

A large SUV on Wilkes left started moving into his lane, attempting to make room where there was none. Wilkes leaned on his horn and yelled at the driver through his window. That got him a one-finger salute. Angry at being held hostage by the traffic jam, Wilkes rolled his window down and motioned for the SUV's driver to do the same.

Frowning, Wilkes flipped his siren and flashed his badge at the belligerent SUV owner. The SUV's window went up quickly, and the driver slowly returned to the middle of his own lane. Yeah, that's right bitch, Wilkes said to himself. He sank back into the seat, picked up his now stone-cold coffee, and took a sip. He said a silent prayer that Mayo wouldn't do anything stupid that would jeopardize the case. Or his own safety. His phone rang. He flipped it over, hit the speaker, and left it on the seat.

"Hello?"

"Hey, Wilkes. I put your 'prop' on your desk. Weird request, but what do I know? You come in for your interview?" the familiar voice filled the Crown Vic.

"Good ole Bernie. Thanks. Yeah, but I have to move on to something else first."

"So how about a little 'quid pro quo'? I have a little time right now and could use the distraction. What's going on?" Bernice said, chuckling softly.

Wilkes shook his head. Her request for inside information had come a little faster than usual, but as was typical, Bernie wanted her due on her schedule.

"Well, seeing as how I'm stuck in traffic, I guess I could let you in on a few details. Providing it's between you, me, and the fence post."

"Like that's ever been an issue? Please! Come on buddy you know the rules; cross the river and pay the ferry."

"You're a fairy...?"

"Funny. If you keep that up, you'll need to find another lackey to do your busy work. Come on, give it up."

"Okay, okay, you win."

Laughing, Wilkes started filling Bernice in on some of the details of the past 24 hours.

Chapter Fifteen:

Seattle, Washington

Brad opened the door, and Larry quickly staggered in. He looked awful. Unshaven, hair uncombed, and looking like he was still in the same clothes he had on last night. The cold weather, and a lack of sleep, had leached all the color from his face, emphasizing his two-day-old beard and bloodshot eyes. His overcoat was wet and soiled. Brad caught a whiff of BO and ammonia as Larry passed him.

"Larry, you're a mess, man. What's up? What's wrong?" Brad asked, struggling to pass off his reaction as naturally as he could.

Looking around the apartment as though expecting to see someone else, Larry jerked his head back and forth and leaned his body awkwardly to and fro as though attempting to improve the angle of his view.

"You alone here, Brad?" He asked, licking his lips nervously.

"Yes, Larry, I'm alone. We're alone. Have you slept since last night? What's your deal?"

Walking over to the wrap-around windows, Larry strained as he looked out on the street. First to the South and then the North. He leaned against the windows, supporting himself with his hand placed against the glass. Shaking his head, he sagged slightly before speaking again.

"Yeah, alone." He turned and faced Brad. "I forgot what a great view you have up here. It must be weird on a day like this, though, huh? Looks almost as if the storm could just...blow right in." He gave Brad a sickly smile.

"Sit down, man. You're freaking me out. You said you were in trouble, and you look like hell. Is this about last night?"

"Last night? What'd you say?"

Brad took a deep breath. He was done being talked at.

"Larry, I'm going to ask you one more time to tell me what you're all messed up over, and if I don't get an answer in about...oh, five seconds, I'm going to throw your ass out!"

"Easy, easy, Brad. I'm good. I mean, I'm not good, but I'll tell you. I'm just kind of having a hard time here, okay?" He shambled over to the chair Wilkes had been sitting in earlier; glancing at the back of the chair and frowning slightly, he flopped down into it.

"You've got 30 seconds, man."

"Okay! Okay! Geez! Give me a break, will you? I've been wandering around for hours. I didn't know where to go. I didn't know what to do." He could see Brad getting ready to start counting again. "Nat's dead, man. I found her when I got home. I thought she was cheating on me, and now this. Maybe the guy she was seeing did it."

So, there it was, thought Brad. He felt a tightening in his throat and a lead weight descending into his stomach. Now it was real.

Carefully moving to the couch, Brad took a seat. Larry watched him, seeming to analyze his reaction. He slowly looked around the condo again. His gaze stopped at the beer bottle on the counter and then returned to Brad.

"What are you saying, Larry? What do you mean dead? Did you call the police, and why did you come here, for fucks sake? What did you come HERE for?"

Relaxing slightly, apparently reassured by Brad's response, Larry leaned back and let out a shaky sigh. "She's dead. Murdered. She's...she's all cut. She's cut up, man."

"Why haven't you called the police, Larry? You need to call them right now."

Larry's head reappeared, and he sprang out of the chair. He stood staring at Brad, swaying slightly.

"I never said I hadn't called the cops. How'd you know that?"

"What? You said you were in trouble and didn't know what to do...I just..."

"You just what? Guessed? Is that what you were going to say? You look nervous all of a sudden old buddy. Why is that?" Larry frowned at Brad.

Swallowing, Brad stood up too and tried to diffuse the situation. He would try to quash Larry's suspicions by coming at him head-on.

"Sit back down, Larry. I mean it. You're not coming into my house, telling a story like that to me, and then playing it off like somehow, I'm at fault. Sit down!"

"Don't try that shit on me, Brad. We played poker together. I've seen you do that to other guys for years. It doesn't work for me. Just what have you been up to today? Somebody else has been here. I know it! Who've you been talking to?" Jutting his jaw forward and scowling at Brad, with his hand in his coat pocket.

After years of bar brawls, and dealing with the occasional muscle-bound malcontent, Brad felt rather than saw what was coming. Moving forward quickly, he stepped on Larry's left foot with his right, pinning him to the floor, and chopped with his left hand at Larry's right elbow. He hit Larry's arm with a thunderous blow. Howling with pain, Larry tried to move away, but because his foot was trapped, he began to fall backward. Pushing and spinning him as he fell, Brad forced him back into the chair face-first. Grabbing Larry's right hand, Brad pulled it painfully up behind his back and put his knee into Larry's back.

"Ow! What are you doing, man! Get off me!" Larry yelled.

"Let's just see what you've got in your pocket, 'old buddy.' You think you can you come to my house and take me? What have you been up to?!" Throwing him onto the floor and keeping his right arm pinned, Brad fumbled in Larry's coat pocket. His fingers came in contact with cold, heavy metal and closed on it. Drawing out his hand, he pulled out a handgun.

"You little SHIT! I should use this on you. That would be the end of it!" Brad grated out through clenched teeth.

In a low voice, Larry beckoned, "Yeah? Why don't you?"

Keeping the pressure on the arm and putting his knee into his back again, Brad forced Larry flat on the floor. Tucking the gun into his pants at the small of his back, Brad took his free hand and dragged Larry's coat down over his shoulders, effectively trapping his arms at his sides. When he felt reasonably sure that he had control of him, Brad pulled him up and marched him into his kitchen. Pulling open a cupboard, he retrieved a roll of duct tape. He pushed Larry ahead of him to the dining area, sat him in one of the chairs, and started taping him to it. Larry was securely strapped into the chair after several minutes and most of the roll of tape later.

After attempting to taunt Brad without success, Larry bowed his head and closed his eyes.

Unwilling to break the silence between them, Brad walked over to the counter, slid onto a stool, and grabbed the beer he had put out earlier. Raising it to his lips, he took a long swig and let it soak his dry throat. Glancing at Larry and reassuring himself that he was still secure, Brad raised the bottle for another mouthful just as the doorbell rang. Hopefully, that was the Cavalry, with Wilkes running point. Brad wanted Wilkes to come in and take his one-time friend off to jail so he could get himself stupid drunk and sleep for a day.

Slipping off the stool, he made his way over to the security system. The screen showed two uniformed officers and Detective Wilkes standing outside his condo door. He forcefully wrenched open the door, surprising the three men waiting outside in the hall.

"Hello, boys. Come right on in. I've got a present for you."

Wilkes frowned, "What the hell, Mayo? A present? The only present I want is your friend wrapped up and tied with a bow!"

Looking Wilkes right in the eyes, Brad said, "Well then, this oughta be...almost perfect."

Chapter Sixteen:

Unknown Place

"What do you mean there's no bathroom?"

"Sorry, Rafe. No toilet. Look around."

Jack indicated the room's expanse with a wave of his hand. Looking very uncomfortable, Rafe looked from Jack to the others.

"Seriously? Are you kidding? What have you been doing when you needed to go?"

Trying not to laugh, Maddy said, "That's what we've been trying to tell you. We haven't needed to go."

"Well, I do! Like real soon. So, unless we all want to see an embarrassing mess, we need to pound on that door over there and get your gold alien to show me the toilet!"

"Won't embarrass me, dude. Just go behind a chair in one of the corners." Daniel grinned.

"That's just perfect! No food and no crapper!" Frustrated, Rafe threw himself into an empty chair.

"Hasn't seemed to bother us." Daniel said and then noticed Rafe's expression, "kidding dude. Just kidding."

The surfer, who had identified himself as Fletcher Fairfield, looked at Rafe's discomfort detachedly. "I don't need to go to the bathroom. Yet. But I am hungry. What do you think they plan on feeding us?" He looked at Jack expectantly, raising an eyebrow.

"Beats me. But Healer said that our care and safety were his concern, so...I guess it's just a matter of time until he realizes we have other needs. Knocking on the door might not be a bad idea. Can't hurt, right?"

Rafe jumped up, went to the door, and slapped his palm against it twice. "Hey! Two more of us are awake, and we want to make your acquaintance!"

Looking back at the others, who were all staring at him with amusement, he said, "What? Just trying to move this thing along. Know what I mean? Plus, is waiting going to change anything?" He rejoined the group and took a seat, carefully crossing his legs.

Looking at the group seated around him, Jack considered their situation for the hundredth time. The bathroom question had come up before but hadn't been of great concern because there hadn't been any pressing need. Food was another matter. He hadn't been hungry or thirsty, but now that he was thinking about it, he was developing a desire for both. Looking about the room and casually inspecting the furnishings, he was once again impressed with the familiar yet alien nature of everything present. The walls seamlessly met the floor. The ceiling-to-wall abutment was more challenging to assess due to the room's great height, but he felt sure it was the same. Although apparently upholstered in leather, the furniture had no seams, rivets, or stitching to indicate how it had been assembled. That had initially creeped out Maddy, but ultimately, she had surrendered to the situation when it had come time to sleep. So, if a bathroom were to be created, would it just spring forth from the floor like a mushroom? Or would the hallway beyond the door lead to an answer for that and the question of food? Jack was anxious for a Healer or another of his race to appear.

In Jack's opinion, the jury was out on whether Fletcher had been a welcome addition to their little group. He had begrudgingly forgiven Daniel but had not extended an olive branch. That made Daniel feel even worse, and Jack felt for his new friend. Like Daniel, Fletcher had been shocked at the lack of injury he had sustained. Before blacking out, he was sure he had suffered some severe internal damage. Noticing Daniel's wincing over that observation, he commented that while he might owe his survival to Daniel, that didn't excuse Daniel's passive role while he was beaten. It had been an awkward moment for the group, but Fletcher seemed oblivious to the mood he had created.

Vacationing in Hawaii alone, using his parent's condo, Fletcher had been picking new spots to surf until his unfortunate meeting with Daniel's friends. His upbringing had been very privileged and had apparently left him with a sense of entitlement. Brought up in a wealthy family in Connecticut, educated at Brown University, and already an executive at his father's business, he was the poster child for the rich and famous with the almost inevitable attitude. Tall, fit, and a strong jawline created an almost movie-star quality to his appearance.

Fletcher believed that his disappearance would not be noticed for a while since he had been traveling alone. Still, once it was, he felt certain that significant influence and power would be applied to a search and his recovery. My parents tend to run over people and take control whenever they can manufacture the slightest cause. Obviously intelligent and curious about their surroundings, he had asked all the now familiar questions. However, he had displayed an aloofness and self-possession that insulated him from the group. When Maddy asked him why he seemed so withdrawn, he said, 'he was just turning it over to God'. Jack had been surprised at that because the declaration of faith seemed disconnected from everything else about him.

Fletcher's composure had been in marked contrast to Rafe's manic behavior.

Rafe was Portuguese, born and raised in California, and raised in the foster care system. Expressive and tending toward the dramatic, he was fun to watch and listen to while he was telling a story. His self-deprecating style was disarmingly funny but so smooth it seemed practiced, and Jack felt confident Rafe was accustomed to being the life of the party. He had been in and out of several youth institutions as a boy, and he had been a transient member of so many foster homes that he claimed to be unable to recall the names of any of his foster parents. He had been very successful at an early age in the music industry as a songwriter. A high-pressure job, a fiancée 'in the business,' a high-maintenance client list, and too much money had gotten him in over his head. And he had, in his own words, 'self-destructed with a vengeance.' His lack of artifice made him very likable. He hadn't brought up any history of addictions, and the others had decided not to pry. He had inquired about the life stories of the others, and Jack had volunteered the fact that three of them shared a common ground of abandonment or being orphaned.

Another mystery? Or coincidence? There are no coincidences, Jack thought.

"Hey, heads up. The door's moving again." Whispered Daniel.

All heads turned in the direction of the door. It was indeed moving inward as it had before prior to Healer's entrance. Having witnessed this spectacle before, Jack didn't feel the anxiety or apprehension that he could read in Fletcher's and Rafe's body language. Both had gotten to their feet. Rafe was nervously looking from the receding surface to the faces of the rest of the group and back to the door. Fletcher stood with his arms folded against his chest and stared intently at the opening in the wall.

The silhouetted form that approached did not seem to be Healer. While bipedal and human in its basic form, it was markedly different even at the distance it had entered the hallway.

First, it did not appear to be much taller than an ordinary person. Secondly, it was giving off light that was so bright that it was painful to look at. The luminescence made it impossible to make out any other details until the figure had entered the room. Upon entering the room, the painful glow abated, allowing details to become more easily discerned. Instead of the loose-fitting garments, Healer had worn; this figure wore armor. Tall but not overwhelmingly, so it was clad in a black-colored metal. The head and hands were exposed, making it clear that the suit of armor was a covering of some kind and not its skin. It would have been hard to discern otherwise due to the form-fitting nature of the metallic sheath. The joints were articulated but not in a metal-work fashion familiar to Jack. Instead of hinges or clumsy nested fittings, the elbows, knees, and shoulders were covered with a series of small sliding disks that constantly shifted to accommodate movement. The feet were encased in the same metal, but the soles must have been some sort of synthetic or soft material as minimal sound had been audible while the figure walked toward them. The face shared many of the Healer's attributes except for the hair and eyes. Metallic strands of silver framed the head, and eyes of startling royal blue with normal pupils at their center stared out from the face. A wide and reassuring smile split the strong countenance.

"I am so glad to be with you." the voice, though solid and deep, did not have the same booming power of Healer's.

Whether from shock or nervousness, they all stared speechlessly. Except for Rafe.

"Dude, you're...not what I was expecting...but where's the can?" he asked, his voice rising slightly.

"Can? Why would you need a can?" The stranger asked in a bemused fashion.

Rafe, seeming ready to burst, practically shouted, "The toilet! A toilet! The head, commode, latrine, outhouse, bidet! Take your pick! Where are we supposed to piss?"

Smiling, the armored man said, "Ah. There." He pointed to the furthest corner of the room.

Five heads turned in unison to stare in open-mouthed amazement. Where only smooth surfaces had existed moments before, a doorway now yawned, light streaming from within. Practically running, Rafe rushed to the door and disappeared inside. The group heard a muffled 'hallelujah' from within the new antechamber and did not attempt to hide their smiles.

"You are all in need of refreshment, I am certain. But first, come and be seated. You have questions, and I will provide some answers. My name is Leiru." Leiru moved gracefully to a chair but waited for the others to follow suit before sitting.

Jack and Maddy chose a nearby couch while the others sat in chairs. When everyone had established themselves, Leiru looked toward the newly created doorway, obviously waiting for Rafe to return. A moment later, the Californian appeared with mock relief written large across his face.

"Whoa, sorry folks, didn't mean to hold up the show. I'll just take my seat and be quiet now." He said as he sat on the couch, sliding in next to Maddy. She edged away slightly, putting her hand on Jack's knee, grimacing in mock distaste for Rafe's behavior.

Leiru had remained standing and did not seat himself. Instead, he began to speak, walking as he did so, looking at each of the humans placed before him.

"You will be sent back to where you were taken very soon. I am sorry that you have agonized over your displacement. I am prepared to spend some time to address your concerns, answer some of your questions and give you some insight as to why you were chosen."

He looked at Jack and smiled. "Each of you is unique and special to our purpose. Each of you were chosen because, at a specific moment, you will have the opportunity to save many of your own kind. Depending upon how you accept your individual roles, you may become an active part of our plan and work with us," he looked away from Jack and Maddy and glanced toward Fletcher, "or you may choose paths that limit your role but will serve our commission nonetheless."

"We have been watching homo sapiens for centuries. Your kind is more important to the universe than you realize. Therefore, we were tasked with binding our enemy to protect you. But now they have escaped and have been wreaking havoc that will destroy billions if they are not stopped. They will come in the guise of saviors but mislead you. They will claim knowledge and power beyond your current experience, and while that is true, they will lie about its origin and intentions. Their goal is to create disorder while professing to bring harmony and peace. They loathe you, your existence, and desire nothing less than to subvert all of your best efforts. Some proxies will be so subtle in their deception that you may not recognize it. Others will be so bold that their imposture will seem evident to you, while others of your kind will deny it. Even while you are here in the safety of this chamber, hundreds of the enemy have inserted themselves into your trusts, your syndicates of power and authority. Those you know and trust may turn against you and may have been working to further these intentions for years without even knowing that they are assisting those of whom I speak."

Stealing a glance at the others, Jack saw his anxiety and confusion mirrored in their faces.

"The preparation Healer spoke of is twofold. The first, nearly complete, is to fortify you for strength and resilience in battle, but different from the kind of physical contest you might envision. You have been changed in ways that are not definable by your science but will not harm you in any fashion. These changes will become obvious to you when you need them. The second is to forewarn you, as I am doing now. I cannot provide specific or detailed delineations as the enemy will disguise itself and take many different routes as it seeks to further its goals. But you will be forearmed and girded by awakening you to the storm that approaches. The protection we have afforded by bringing you here was to remove you from dangerous paths at moments that were critical for each of you. While the others do not know you by name, they know the quiescent nature and probable location for the obstacles to their success that you each represent."

Striding with a smooth grace that seemed supernatural, Leiru walked to a chair and sat. His face was severe but encouraging, and he continued.

"When you are returned, you will almost assuredly be questioned about this experience. Our Leader has instructed us to leave your memories of your time here intact. But know this, should you elect to corrupt our intention, you will be dealt with harshly. Intentional disobedience and insurrections will not be tolerated. You cannot deny your participation. You are tools and can only blunt your ability to impact the outcome, but you cannot remove yourself from involvement. You may even discover that combining your gifts and resources can make you more effective in thwarting the enemy. But when you share your experience with others, recognize that there will be skepticism, derision, and retaliatory behaviors with which to contend."

Glancing at each of them, waiting for them to digest what he had told them. He favored them with a warm and reassuring smile.

"The giants that abducted each of you are called Nephilim. They have lived in your world for thousands of years. They seek to serve us as a means of discharging an ancient encumbrance and freeing themselves from an alliance with the enemy. While it is unlikely that you will see them again, they should be considered allies and trusted to protect you and serve us." Putting his hands on his armored knees, he leaned forward and grinned.

"What other queries might you have before I take my leave?"

"When's dinner?" Rafe asked.

"You got any Lau Lau?" Daniel chuckled.

A wry smile creased Leiru's face, and he waved a hand, indicating the space behind them. Turning to see what he was pointing at, the group saw a table piled high with fruit, cheeses, bread, and decanters of liquid.

Tempting, Jack thought, but he was more interested in hearing more from Leiru. He could tell that some others were having difficulty controlling themselves and was considering how to encourage them to wait when Fletcher spoke up.

"Wow, that is quite an impressive trick. But I, for one, would like to ask a few questions before we 'break bread.' Is that acceptable, Leiru?" he asked.

"Yes." The silver-maned man nodded and spoke kindly.

Clearing his throat, Fletcher began, "I am the only one here who was taken without seeing your henchmen, but the others have described them to me. Are you of a completely different species, and why is it that you and Healer, whom I have not met, look so human and yet are clearly not human. Where are you from?"

Piercing blue eyes appraised Fletcher as Leiru considered his answer.

"Direct. Our history is intertwined, but as you see us now, we are true of different races. Healer and I have modified our appearance so that you may associate our form with familiar and unthreatening images. We often change our manifested forms because our pure forms would be difficult, if not dangerous, to look upon for some of you."

My God! Thought Jack. What could they look like in their natural aspect? What could be so fearsome that it could be dangerous? "What could be so frightening, so devastating that just to look at it could cause injury?" Jack asked.

Leiru paused again before responding, "Some things about us, our nature, and our facets cannot be easily explained. They are integral to our past; we are not yet ready to disclose our origin. In their purest manifestation, some of our forms exceed your ability to safely comprehend. I do not know why this is. It just IS."

"Yeah, yeah, yeah. It is what it is, right? What about those crazy rocks your boys used on us? What are those? And why did it fuck up my shirt without hurting me?" Rafe asked. Confusion played across his face.

"The 'rocks' are brethren, just as Healer is, even though we are of different castes. They are called Orphans. Neither weapon, nor instrument, they are living beings whose natural form is exactly as you have seen them. They have cooperated with the Nephilim to ensure and aid your safe liberation. They are sentient and imbued with great power that they can modulate. Any force they employ is controlled by them specific to their purpose. Your shirt was damaged because it is comprised of non-living materials."

Something about this conversation was bothering Jack. He felt like there was an answer or understanding beyond his reach. Something he knew but could not remember.

"What about the Nephilim? Is that what you call them?" Maddy asked, leaning forward. "Some of us thought they might resemble statues on an island in the Pacific. Is that where they are from?"

"Ahh, the idols. Those carvings were indeed the work of the Nephilim, though they would be ashamed to be reminded of them. The island you refer to was once home to them, but they have not resided there for many years."

"Why? I mean...why would they be ashamed? Why would they...why did they leave?" She asked.

Leiru stared hard at Maddy, attempting to see beneath or through her question.

"The answers are both tied together. The monoliths you refer to were built by the Nephilim. They were grandiose monuments to themselves. They worshipped their own image. Their indulgence was ironic in that it was exactly the same behavior that had caused them to be banished and the reason for their brutish appearance. They would be ashamed to have you recognize them from the stone images on that island because it represented a time in their long-ago history when they had abased themselves."

Maddy breathed slowly, "Practically everything you say is so convoluted or vague that it just creates more questions for us. Can't you just say it straight out? I mean, really! How did they leave the island? And if they are ashamed, then there must be some social, cultural, or spiritual basis for their shame. What would that be? You don't just run around on an island doing whatever you want and suddenly have an epiphany that what you're doing is inappropriate. There must be a catalyst. So, what was it? You?"

Blue eyes sparkling with delight, Leiru smiled at Maddy.

"So impetuous. No, the impetus for the Nephilim's shame and regret was not due to me, at least not me alone. Rather, it was all my kind and the one to whom we all answer. And it was the Nephilim's remembrance of a time when they were close to realizing their potential. Before they succumbed to the corruption of their own conception. And to answer your other question regarding their history, they did not leave the island. They were taken."

Shaking her head, Maddy sighed and looked at the ceiling in frustration. Jack felt her aggravation just as keenly. The others were focused on Leiru and noticeably needed help to absorb the details of the conversation. Was his entire dialogue just a means of clouding the true nature of their abduction and roles in some upcoming conflict? Why was he being so indirect? Was it deliberate?

"Why are you being so obtuse, Leiru?" Fletcher asked. "Why pretend to answer our questions if the only answers you are willing to give us are vague and generalized? A 'storm' is coming? Save billions of our kind? That sounds like bad theater or a ridiculously cheap contrivance."

Leiru's brows drew together, eyes flashing as his lips formed a frown.

"Take care. An insult to me is an insult to my Captain. And I will not tolerate any disrespect."

Swallowing hard but refusing to give ground, Fletcher remained where he stood, even though he apparently wanted nothing more than to step away from Leiru. Jack looked at the others and decided to step into the break-in conversation.

"Leiru, you demand respect, and clearly, you and Healer have the superior position here, but you must see that from our perspective, the only questions we have are the ones you created. You aren't clearly answering any of them. So, with no disrespect intended, why are you being so...ambiguous?" As he spoke, Maddy leaned against him and touched his arm lightly.

Eyes still focused upon an uncomfortable Fletcher, Leiru turned away to face Jack. His frown disappeared and was replaced by a smile.

"You are a natural peacemaker." Drawing a deep breath, he raised a hand in a gesture of peace to the rest of the group.

"My answers are constrained by the instructions I have been given as a messenger. My responses to your questions are as complete as I am allowed to make them. By way of explanation, consider this: you wish for a child to participate in an activity because you are aware that it will benefit the child. The activity's nature is such that if the child chooses to participate based upon a reward, the process will cease to have value and, in fact, may become untenable. The child must elect to be involved based solely on faith that the activity is valuable, not due to an anticipated boon. The analogy is not perfect, but it is the only way in which I can answer your question, which to you must be perceived as elusiveness. It is not, I assure you, a deliberate attempt to deceive you."

"So, if you can't be specific about time, place, who, or what, then why discuss it at all. How does our hazy understanding change things for the better? What does it help?" Jack asked.

Leiru walked over to the table of food and stretched out a hand. Three pieces of fruit rose from the table and hung in midair. Turning back to the group, he said, "I will send this fruit toward the three of you. I will not tell you exactly when that will occur. Watch."

Everyone watched the levitating fruit warily, looking at Leiru for any advance warning.

A moment or two went by, seeming to stretch out into agonizingly uncomfortable minutes. Without any outward change in Leiru's stance, the fruit suddenly sped in opposite directions. Jack caught a pear before it struck his shoulder, Fletcher grabbed an orange as it flew toward his head, and an apple thunked harmlessly into Rafe's chest, falling into his lap.

"Ouch?" Rafe said, obviously unhurt.

Jack looked at the fruit he had caught and then handed it to Maddy. He looked back to Leiru questioningly.

"The intent was to show you what warning you may have that things are about to change. You were prepared but only partially. Even in this limited sense, not all of you were successful in catching the fruit. There may be even less warning and less specificity when encountering the adversary. And I do not share precise details simply because we do not need to, they just are. We can warn you about specific threats in some instances, but I don't know when that might be.

"Oh, my gosh! This is so good!" Biting into his apple, Rafe exclaimed. Juices dripped down his chin as he took another bite.

Maddy groaned and rolled her eyes, "Can you focus?"

Daniel got up, walked to the table, and took two pears, tossing one to Jack as he reseated himself.

"So, we're forewarned, fortified in some way to protect us. But what are we expected to do when you return us, and how do we know that your intentions are truly benign?" he asked.

Standing before them, his blue eyes focused intently, Leiru responded.

"You are expected to do what you believe you should do. You are destined for the situations you will encounter, but your choices after that are up to you. As to our benevolence? That you will have to accept on faith, or not at all. As I have told you, the more you know, the more your choices will be influenced or tainted. It will not serve our purposes."

Jack sighed and took an experimental bite of the pear. It was incredibly delicious. Jack wasn't sure if he had ever tasted a pear that was as sweet. He was past wondering about the how of it all and had come to accept their extraordinary circumstances. But the unpredictable impact on his future, their future, weighed on him.

"We return home, I'm guessing, the same way that we arrived. Seeing as we were all unconscious, I'm hoping that won't be necessary for the return trip. When do we leave? And where is your Captain? Aren't we going to meet him? What other preparations are we slated for?"

Leiru looked at Jack with something close to kindness.

"So many countless questions. Your departure will depend upon timing. You will be conscious when you leave, not that it will allow you to observe your travel. The other preparations will be concluded when Healer has visited you once more. And as to the Captain, he keeps his own counsel. He will meet with you when it suits him and no sooner."

Jack looked up from his pear, "Thank you for the food. So, if I summarized all of this, stated the thesis of the moment as it were, the bottom line is we go back, we're expected to 'step up to the plate' so to speak when the bad guys show up, but we can't tell anyone about you, and," he glanced around the room, "all this. Then what? Is there some singular event that we're involved in? Then it, us, our involvement, is over? Or, as you said earlier, do we become part of some action that you and your...people will continue with? And if that's true, do we get some sort of contact or communication from you, from your Captain?"

Looking at Jack and then Fletcher with a noncommittal expression, Leiru said, "As 'vague' as you may feel this sounds, all of those questions will be answered by each of you and will depend upon the choices you make."

Still standing and holding his uneaten orange, Fletcher frowned.

"There is no debating the fact that we are in extraordinary circumstances. Your abilities, your power over us, and your surroundings are inarguable. But I can't make some sort of oath of fealty or commitment to support your efforts based on what you've told us. You've healed me. And I Thank you. I am definitely grateful for that. You haven't harmed us, but you have decided to 'change' us somehow without our permission. How could you respect our agreement to help you, or at least not hinder you, when we would be making that decision based on what little you have told us? I believe in a higher power. A power that has dominion over everything. Even you. You can count me out."

The air in the room seemed charged with electricity as Fletcher finished speaking. Leiru's face took on a somber expression at Fletcher's words. Jack looked at each of the others in turn and could tell that Fletcher's comments had resonated with them but not to the extent of motivating them to speak up. It seemed as though they were all waiting for Jack to speak. Why would that be the case? What informal bond had been formed that seemed to designate him as their unofficial spokesman? Jack stood, and the others slowly got to their feet as well.

"Leiru, Fletcher has a point, although I don't know whether I agree with the way he said it." Fletcher's frown deepened at this.

"But if we take a pragmatic view of what's happened already and the fact that, at least at this point in time, we have no control over the outcome, we are probably resigned to fulfill the roles your plan has already designated for us. Does that satisfy you?"

Leiru had listened impassively as Jack spoke. The sadness had not left his face.

"No, it does not satisfy me. Nor will it please my Captain, but it is an honest answer. There is no room here for pragmatism. We will not force any of you to do our bidding. The level of your participation in the events that are about to unfold is entirely up to you. We are counting on some of you making the leap of faith necessary to join us fully in our battle." He glanced at Fletcher. "Your disbelief and lack of trust sadden me. But I cannot blame you or any of the others for having reservations. All I can ask is that you entertain the possibility of changing your decision."

He extended his hand toward the table. "Eat. I will take my leave, and Healer will join you in a while. Save any other questions for him." And with that, he turned and began walking toward the hallway that led out of the room.

Fletcher took a few steps toward him and reached out to place a hand on Leiru's armored shoulder. As he came close to making contact, a blue and white flash erupted in the air between his hand and Leiru's armor, forcing his hand away and causing him to stumble backward.

Leiru turned quickly.

"You cannot touch us without our permission. Do not attempt it again. What did you wish?"

Cradling his hand with the other, Fletcher took another step back.

"I want to walk with you. You don't have the right. I want to see the rest of the ship. I don't want to be confined in this room any longer. I demand..."

"Stop!" commanded Leiru.

"What you want at this moment is of no interest to us! Make no demands upon us. We do not answer YOU! You will remain here until we send you back. You are filled with boorishness and arrogance! You are so close and yet so distant from the truth." He turned away again.

"I know what the truth is!" Fletcher shouted. "And you aren't part of it!"

Not willing to accept what was clearly a dismissal, Fletcher followed behind Leiru. As Leiru approached the opening, the luminescence emanating from him that had dimmed upon his entrance to the room began gaining brilliance and strength as he moved into the hallway. At first, Fletcher attempted to shield his eyes with his hands, then closed them entirely as he continued blindly stumbling after Leiru. Finally, at the hall's threshold, he fell to his knees. Looking away from the intense light spilling from the hallway, Jack went to him, knelt, and placed a hand on his back.

"Fletcher, are you okay?" he asked as Maddy, Daniel, and Rafe rushed up behind them.

His shoulders shaking, head down, Fletcher struggled to speak, "I...too bright...even with my eyes closed...like looking into the sun."

Jack looked up to the hallway. The door had already closed.

Chapter Seventeen:

SEATTLE WASHINGTON

Outside, the storm continued with fury. Rain hammered at the windows, trees shook violently, and yet, no sound penetrated the condo's walls. Wilkes and the two uniformed officers stood in Brad's kitchen. Their clothes dripping on the hardwood floor, staring at a silent and sullen Larry Ellsworth.

Glaring at the two uniformed officers, Wilkes cleared his throat.

"You want to tell me again how I almost beat the two of you here when I was driving from West Seattle, and you were just on the other side of the 5?"

"We got a call on a 030 in progress. Seemed more important than," he glanced at the securely taped Ellsworth, "your little issue here," the taller of the two patrolmen retorted. He locked eyes with Wilkes and belligerently refused to back down.

"Yeah? How'd that work out? Wrap that up quickly, did you...Turner?" Wilkes sneered, using the officers name, visible on his nameplate. "There is no way an armed robbery could be resolved that quickly."

"You know, weirdest thing, it was a false alarm or prank. Doesn't matter. We had to respond." Brad watched the cop's face get redder as he fumed.

"Besides, looks like someone did your work for you anyway, DETECTIVE. Nice job, Mr. Mayo."

"Whatever, TURNER. Thanks for nothing. I got this; you two can return to saving the world, or whatever you were doing," said Wilkes as he took a deep breath and exhaled.

Wilkes turned his back on the officers, passively dismissing them, and walked toward Larry. Brad feeling a little awkward in the situation, decided to walk the officers out.

"Those fuckin' guys pissed me off so bad. They couldn't get here any faster than me, and I was at your place in West Seattle when I heard you were here." Wilkes said to Larry.

He stared down at Larry as though imploring him to talk. He had been read his rights and grunted his understanding but had not offered any other sound or acknowledgment.

"You going to play it that way?" Wilkes asked. "Talk to me; it will all be over faster. No long, drawn-out legal process. Better for everybody here."

Larry slowly raised his head. A wicked grin spread across his face.

"Better for you, you mean. You got a date with a six-pack and a bucket of chicken that you need to get back to? You limp Dick." Larry said with a chuckle.

"Yeah, sure do. And go ahead, do that. Be a smart ass. There are ways to make this whole process even more unpleasant than it already is. I've got forensics headed over here, and they're going to go over your wife's car. And they're going to find something you missed. You can earn some goodwill points by cooperating, or you can be a pain in the ass and just make it harder on yourself. That what you want?"

Larry leaned back in the chair and flipped his hair out of his face with a shake of his head.

"What do I want? Let's see...I want my wife's killer brought to justice. I want to be spared from having to talk lowbrow idiots like you. I want my tax dollars to be spent on improving the city infrastructure instead of being wasted on a good dental plan for fat, badly dressed jackasses who couldn't get a real job and ended up being a cop. Ohh, sorry...I meant limp Dick. And...what else...oh, yeah...I want to be NOT considered responsible for my wife's death because I didn't do anything to hurt her!" Larry smirked as he finished, but the smile quickly disappeared as Brad walked into the room.

Fighting to keep his mounting anger under control, Wilkes growled at Larry, "You sick...you want me to believe that you found your wife dead over ten hours ago and during all that time never thought to call the police? You aren't really thinking this through, are you? You're in custody. You're going to be charged with murder, and you want to trade insults and offer that weak BS as your defense?"

Larry adopted a more subdued attitude and said, "Takes two to trade, doesn't it? And call you? That worked out Ohh so well last night, didn't it? We try to help some girls that are being attacked in an alley and we get knocked out in the process. Then, for our troubles, we get blamed for the mugging and grilled for hours. Yeah, you guys were the first people I thought about calling. If those freaks can follow

126

me home somehow and do what they did to Nat, I figure I'm working from a short list of people I can trust to protect me." Looking at Brad, he added in a louder voice, "And apparently, that list is shorter than I thought."

"Screw you, Larry," said Brad. "You tried to pull a gun on me. You're not guilt-tripping me. I hope you rot in prison, you little shit."

"Screw me? I'm the one getting screwed, alright. What did you expect me to do? I find Nat dead...cut to...pieces. I try to come here and get help from my friend, but you've already convicted me. Then, you set me up to have the cops arrest me. I haven't done anything wrong. I'm scared. You're supposed to be my friend."

"You didn't act so hurt and innocent a few minutes ago." Wilkes said.

"I don't know what you're talking about." Larry responded flatly.

Rubbing his face, Wilkes squared his shoulders and walked over to Larry. "Okay, smart guy. I'll just un-tape you, and we'll finish this at the station." Reaching into his jacket, he pulled out a large folding knife and opened it with a flick of his thumb. "But no telling what might happen while I'm cutting you loose. You know, with you being so uncooperative and violent."

Looking from Wilkes to Brad and back again, Larry appeared uncertain.

"You wouldn't try anything in front of a witness." He said, glancing meaningfully at Brad.

"Oh, you mean the witness you were going to use this on?" Wilkes said, holding up an evidence bag containing the pistol Brad had taken away from Larry.

"I brought that with me for protection. I never intended to use it on Brad. I came here to try and figure things out."

"Yeah? Well, I..." Brad started, then the security system chimed. "It's like Grand Central Station around here today." Brad said with a frustrated sigh.

He walked over to the monitor and saw three men in dark suits standing outside on the ground floor. Tapping a button on the virtual screen, he said, "Yes?"

One of the men stepped up to the monitor, his face filling the screen.

"Mr. Mayo? Samuel Bliss, NSA. We would like to speak with you, please." He stepped back slightly as he spoke and raised an open wallet displaying a laminated ID and badge.

Brad looked back at Wilkes.

"Guy says he's NSA. What's this about?"

"I thought the FBI might weigh in on the kidnapping last night, but who knows?" said Wilkes.

Brad tapped the screen twice and said, "come up to the top floor. I'm in 400."

The three figures on the screen disappeared as they entered the building.

"So, looks like we're having a party." Brad sighed to Wilkes.

"Yeah, well, I've been expecting something like this."

Chapter Eighteen:

UNKNOWN LOCATION

The group had been very animated since Leiru's departure. Fletcher apparently hadn't suffered any permanent injury and seemed to recover from the experience quickly. He had continued to be very vocal about his unwillingness to commit to any kind of support of the extraterrestrials based on the lack of any credible explanation of what 'events' were impending. Rafe was noncommittal and indifferent. Jack, Maddy, and Daniel had debated their personal views on what it all meant. They were conversing while eating the food that Leiru had provided. Everyone had taken a seat, pulling chairs into a rough circle. Everyone except Fletcher. He remained standing and was trying to inspire some kind of response from Rafael.

"Don't you care? You're kidnapped and fed unsubstantiated garbage, and you're comfortable just sitting there eating food that came from who knows where? What we think we're seeing or experiencing doesn't agree with thousands of years of Christian history!" The veins in Fletcher's neck stood out as he spoke.

Looking up lazily from his sprawled position, with one leg over the arm of his chair, Rafael smiled. "You always this intense? How Christian is that? Isn't there some rule in the good book about not losing control? I'm not fatalistic, but our situation doesn't seem to give us any alternatives other than going with the flow. You know?"

"Being Christian doesn't mean being a doormat! What were you before they brought you here? A complete burnout? Anyone with half a brain would be completely unwilling to listen to, let alone accept, the vague load of crap that...thing tried to pass off. We shouldn't just sit here and submissively accept anything they have to say. Where's the proof? There are no such things as aliens. This isn't God's hand, either, although I wish it was. What's the real purpose here? Why should we agree to cooperate at all?" said Fletcher, as his eyes narrowed, and he jabbed a finger in the air, pointing at Rafe.

The others stopped talking and focused their attention on the brewing argument.

"Dude. Just because I'm not wound as tight as you doesn't mean there isn't anything going on beneath the surface. It also doesn't mean I can't get up and kick your ass right now. So, you need to take that voice down a notch and watch the way you talking to me. You and the others all heard my story. Yeah, I've been on the loser end of life for a while, and I might not be as well educated as you, Mr. Ivy league. But I wouldn't call our abductions, the obvious power of our captors, and the amazing sleight of hand here that can produce cheese, juice, and...Bathrooms from thin air unsubstantiated. You're looking for proof? Assurance? Clarity? How about this: if they wanted to hurt us or brainwash us or subvert us in some alien fashion, why haven't they? I'm willing to let this play out because I'm not hurt, being fed, and frankly, I feel pretty damn good."

Fletcher's eyes narrowed.

"You think you're tough? You're articulate. I'll give you that. But don't threaten me. I'm pretty sure I could take you."

The others took a collective step back as Rafe slowly stood up.

Rafe stood with his arms loosely at his sides.

"Thinking and doing are two different things." He said to Fletcher.

"What?"

"You said you THINK you can take me, but doing it is something different. You're basing your opinion on little scuffles you may have had at your fancy-ass schools or even some piddly martial arts training. But none of that matters if you aren't prepared to go all the way. I don't get into fights. As a rule. Too much can happen, it's unpredictable. But if I do, I'm not distracted thinking about tomorrow. I'm ready to die today, right now." Rafe stared evenly at Fletcher.

"What the hell are you talking about?"

"I'm saying I don't think I like you. And the next time you start mouthing off about how you're going to 'take me,' I'm going to give you a beating that you won't recover from."

Throwing his hands up, Fletcher looked over at the others for support. Finding none, he walked to the far side of the room and flung himself angrily into a chair. No one moved to join him. Rafe sat back down as Jack stood up and walked over to the table to get some fruit.

"Well, guess now that that's over, anyone want another piece of fruit?" said Jack as he took a bite.

He chalked up Fletcher's emotional tirade to the tension they all felt. The confrontation with Leiru had been unsettling. While no one had been injured, it was easy to see why Fletcher felt so emotional. The easy way Leiru dealt with Fletcher was another dramatic example of Leiru and Healer's power. He looked over at Maddy and Daniel, who had resumed their discussion while casting furtive glances at Fletcher. Rafe sighed and looked over to Jack. Raising one eyebrow questioningly, he took a large bite of a banana.

"What's on your mind, fearless leader?"

"Fearless leader? Ha ha, very funny. I don't know what to think. But I don't want you and him screwing around anymore. Let's all try to keep it on the copacetic. Okay?"

Rafe shrugged and leaned back into the chair.

Brushing her hands off on her pants, Maddy stood up. She looked at Jack and pointedly nodded over at Fletcher.

"Well, whether we're making sense of all this or not, we need to stick together. One of us should talk to him."

Jack, Daniel, and Rafe just stared at her.

"Really? None of you are willing to get him to come back over here?"

"Nope!" the three guys responded in unison.

"Just give him some time to get over being butt hurt. Guys process stuff differently. He'll come around." Daniel said as Rafe and Jack smirked.

Maddy crossed her arms over her chest and focused on Jack.

"Jack? I thought you were a little more mature. You're just going to let him stew over there by himself?"

"He really was being a bit of an ass. Let him cool off. Give him a few minutes alone." Jack said as he chewed an orange wedge and tried to focus on Maddy's question instead of how her pose accentuated her figure.

Looking up at the distant ceiling, then casting a withering look at Rafe, Maddy shook her head, spun around, and walked off in Fletcher's direction. Jack wasn't sure how to react to that, so he decided to let it go. Or at least, he tried to let it go. Was that a tingle of jealousy he felt as Maddy sat down with Fletcher? And laid her hand on his shoulder?

What the hell is this?

He forced himself to turn away now facing Daniel and Rafe. Rafe raised his eyebrow again while fighting back a smile. Daniel pretended to be busy inspecting the bread he had been eating.

"What? What?" Jack asked, exasperated.

Rafe laughed and said, "Oh, nothing. Are we experiencing a separation of the troops? Not your girl sitting over there with Mr. Rich Blond Blue Blood."

Daniel laughed. "Nice alliteration. Need to come up with a word for rich that starts with a 'b,' though. And 'bitch' doesn't count. Too easy."

"Blond, Blue, Blood, Blob? You know, bitch does work well for him though," Rafe said.

Making a throat-clearing noise, Jack said, "Stop. Stop it. Both of you. Maddy and I were taken together, and that's it. And I know you can't stand Fletcher, but we all need to get on the same page." He did not look over at Fletcher and Maddy while he was talking.

"Relax, brah. Just joking, yeah? This whole situation is pretty intense. How long can we keep a serious conversation going without a laugh or two? No big thing. As soon as Mr. Richie gets his underwear untangled from his ass, we should be all good." Daniel said raising his hand in a calming gesture.

Rafe was laughing good-naturedly and added, "Yeah, man. No worries. We're just busting your balls a little. But what did you mean you don't know what to think? It's like Close Encounters. Or Transformers, right? They've finally showed up. The aliens. Except it sounds like there's two species or factions or something. And we're caught in the middle. I mean, other than the obviously epic implications, that seems pretty easy to grasp for me."

"Who knows what is really going on here?" Jack said. "Extraterrestrials? I guess that's one answer. But what I meant was this is different from how it's supposed to go. Aliens, I mean. Forget that Fletcher brought it up first, but where is God in all this? Is this part of the end times? I always believed that we're judged, and that's it. I've never bought into the 'life on other planets' stuff. My whole life has been looking at the future in a completely different, realistic, way."

Looking at Jack with a smile, Rafe said, "Yep. It's for sure the Decepticons vs Autobots."

Jack just stared flatly back at Rafe.

Locking his hands behind his head and stretching his legs out, Daniel said, "Mm, yeah. I get that. But what's happening here doesn't necessarily mean that Revelations isn't accurate. We don't know the context for any of this.

How it plays into the future. In fact, we don't even know how it plays into our own lives when and if we go back."

"Please. You're both making my skin crawl. Just tell me you're not going to start quoting scripture." Rafe said rolling his eyes.

"I don't know any scripture for this. But I do wonder how this fits into what I believe. If I pray right now, does God hear me while we're here? I have to believe He does. What power does He hold over Leiru? Or Healer? I'm really struggling with all of this. With everything I've known and believed in." Jack said with more concern on his face.

Sitting up, Daniel looked at Jack.

"Me too. But we have yet to get any answers, just talking it over amongst ourselves, yeah? We need a little input from our 'Keepers.' Whatever they are. Don't stress trying to come up with an explanation based on what little we know."

"You're right. Some of this has to become clear pretty soon. I mean, if there really is some sort of confrontation coming, that alone has to create some definition, some understanding." Jack said.

Rafe stood up, stretched, and walked over to the food-laden table. Picking through the mounds of food, he selected a large wedge of white cheese.

"What I know for certain is that I feel great. Like, I feel rested, strong, and ... clear-headed." Daniel and Jack exchanged glances.

"What? What did I say? I feel good. What's wrong with that?"

Jack looked down at his hands and then back up to make eye contact with Rafe.

"Look, it's none of our business, but Healer mentioned that the reason you and Fletcher took so long to wake up was because he was being healed from being beaten and...you were being...cleansed. So, maybe the reason you feel so good, maybe the way they changed you was they removed or filtered something out that was in your system. He said you had been hurting yourself for a long time."

Daniel made an effort not to look directly at Rafe.

"So? Yeah, man, you're right. It isn't any of your business. But I just don't see any reason to be coy. I've been spending the last couple of years doing a lot of shit, that isn't good for you. You know. Numbing myself. Trying to forget all the stuff I screwed up or lost. No needles. But everything else. Not proud of it. In fact, I was already trashed before I lost my gig in the music biz. That probably was the reason I lost it. And my fiancée. Although, to be completely frank about everything, that isn't your business, and it was a blessing."

Jack and Daniel were silent, feeling awkward and unsure of how to respond.

"Yeah, so I feel good. And at least on the surface, that makes the ET weirdos okay in my book. Until they do something outlandish. Although the way I got taken still bugs me. I mean, isn't there an easier way to abduct people than to send giant thugs to scare the crap out of everybody and take us by force?"

Jack took the question as an opportunity to interject.

"And that brings us right back to square one. We don't know..."

A scream split the air, and all three jumped. Jack whirled in the direction where Maddy and Fletcher had been talking. Maddy was on her feet, hands covering her mouth.

Fletcher was gone.

Chapter Nineteen:

SEATTLE, WASHINGTON

Brad rubbed the back of his neck. Hard. He could feel a serious headache coming on. Too many twists and turns today. Need more sleep. And definitely too many people in my house telling me to jump and how high.

He looked over at the three NSA agents.

"You want to run that by me again? Because I'm not sure I understood you. I just disarmed a man who attempted to pull a gun on me, and you're telling me that you're letting him go? That's bullshit!"

Red-faced and breathing through his mouth, Wilkes took a step back toward the kitchen, blocking the agent's view of Ellsworth.

"You're not taking anything. I've got an open murder investigation, and this dirtbag is good for it. This case will be closed today, and nothing you say will change that."

"We may need to rewind here. You, Detective Wilkes, need clarification. You believe that you have territorial rights that have been violated. Frankly, I find that line of thought ludicrous. And while you may think that nothing, I say can obviate your intentions, your immediate superior certainly can. I suggest you call your captain before making any other statements you will regret later." Said Bliss, the tallest of the three agents.

He looked from Wilkes to Brad, as he exuded calm. His aquiline features and pale skin gave him a refined, somewhat predatory appearance. Close-cropped black hair with silver highlights shone under the condo's overhead lighting. Adjusting the lapel of his black overcoat, Bliss drew himself to his considerable full height. Pale grey eyes focused intently on Wilkes. The two agents standing behind Bliss wore matching tan overcoats and grim smiles. One tall and muscular, the other short and stocky. The taller of the two stared intently at Ellsworth over Wilkes's shoulder, and the short one kept his gaze directed at Brad. Their wet clothing dripped silently on Brad's floor, creating small puddles on the hardwood.

"And you, Mr. Mayo, may feel emboldened because we are standing in your apartment, but you are also confused. We do not recognize any boundaries where National security is concerned. Nor do we, as you inaccurately stated, have any intention of releasing Mr. Ellsworth. At least, not immediately. There are several incidents that have occurred within the last few days that are undoubtedly related. And we have the highest authority empowering us to determine exactly how and what happened."

He nodded to the other agents, who were clearly his subordinates, and they moved slowly toward Wilkes.

"Now, detective, you will stand aside so that agents Dent and Slater can unbind Mr. Ellsworth. And as for you, Mr. Mayo, my thanks for securing Mr. Ellsworth and saving us the time tracking him down ourselves."

His eyes drilled unflinching into Wilkes. Wilkes refused to look away but begrudgingly stepped aside as Dent and Slater walked past him into the kitchen. Digging a hand into his sport coat, Wilkes pulled out his cell and hit a name in his contacts as he stalked angrily over to the windows, his eyes never leaving Bliss.

Brad stared angrily as the NSA agents cut the tape away while Larry watched him from hooded eyes.

"So that's it? He may have killed his wife, tried to attack me, and you're just taking him? Because he might be connected to some of..." Brad paused, unwilling to draw more attention to his presence during the events of the night before.

Bliss's eyes tracked from Larry's unrestraint to Brad's.

"Yes, that's right, Mr. Mayo. We know all about your involvement in matters we are investigating. Rest assured that we are still very interested in speaking with you too."

Wilkes had completed his phone call and loudly grunted as he ended the call. Bliss calmly looked over at him.

"Did you confirm your disposition in this situation, detective?"

Clearly angry, Wilkes just nodded. A vein pulsed in his temple, and his cheeks were red and blotchy with repressed rage.

Ignoring Wilkes's apparent anger, Bliss turned to Dent and Slater. "Mr. Ellsworth, you are now my problem. Agent Dent will restrain you with handcuffs. Should you attempt to be anything less than totally cooperative, you will be sedated. Do not test our resolve. Even once."

Dent pulled Larry's hands behind his back and secured them with plastic cuffs. Satisfied that Larry was under control, Dent and Slater shoved him forcefully toward the front door.

As he approached the door, Bliss put a hand on the doorknob and turned back toward Brad and Wilkes.

"Neither of you have any idea what you have stumbled into." He tugged at the overcoat's lapels again, straightening the lines of his coat and brushing a few remaining drops of moisture onto the floor. "You are advised not to discuss one aspect of this little matter with anyone. I am giving you advance notice of this for your own benefit. Be reckless with this information, and you will find yourselves in a very tight spot."

He turned the knob, opened the door, and walked out, followed quickly by the other agents, who drove a cowed and quiet Larry ahead of them.

Brad moved quickly to the door and slammed it shut. He stood for a moment with his hand on the door. Turning, he looked at Wilkes and shook his head.

"So, what now? I feel like something really wrong just happened here. Is Larry just getting away with this?"

Bowing his head slightly, Wilkes took a deep breath. When he looked back up, his face had regained some of its normal color, but his fury still flashed behind his eyes.

"Over my dead body. Your pal killed his wife. One way or another, he's going down. He'll have a hell of a time getting lawyered up while the NSA have him. And I can't touch him right now either, but when they're done, his ass is mine. He's not getting away with what he did to that woman. And I don't for one second buy his story about the same thugs that kidnapped your other friend as being the ones that murdered his wife. No way." He started walking past Brad toward the door.

Brad felt off balance and deflated. The adrenaline rush from the fight had worn off, and he was starting to feel a little shaky.

"Where are you off to? What happens now?"

Frowning, Wilkes looked hard at Brad. "I'm going to find out how the hell these NSA guys knew I had Ellsworth here. And how two officers on patrol less than four miles away weren't able to get here in under an hour."

"How're you going to do that?"

"Well, to start with, I'm going to make sure CSI still crawls over every inch of Ellsworth's car, and then I'm going to find out who fed the thirty report to dispatch that pulled those two uniforms off my request for assistance. Then, I'm going to talk with the only other people who knew that Ellsworth was in this building. Because the NSA isn't in our network. Officially. Someone had to tip them off. And I also have an interview scheduled with the Johnson girl. You know, the girl we found in the alley with you and Ellsworth."

"I know you shot me down the last time I asked, but can I go with you?"

"Yeah." Said Wilkes without hesitation.

Surprised, Brad said, "Yeah? I mean, don't get me wrong, I'm glad, but why is it okay now where it wasn't before?"

"Because Mayo. Before, I was working the case, following the rules. Crossing 'T's' and dotting 'I's.' Now... this whole investigation, as far as I'm concerned, is off the grid. All bets are off. You might come in handy. You did well with Ellsworth, and besides I could use some unofficial backup. Especially if there's a rat running around the department."

Pulling a huge leather bomber jacket out of the hall closet, Brad pulled it on, frowning.

Wilkes tilted his head to one side.

"What? Are you changing your mind? Don't want to go?"

"No, I'm in. I was just thinking about Bliss. There was something 'off' about that guy."

"Yeah, government badges. They're all arrogant pricks."

"No. Well yeah, I guess. But that's not what I meant. Did you notice how his coat was practically dry? The water just rolled off it. And it's pouring out there. His boys were soaked, but he was barely wet. Doesn't that seem odd to you?"

"Yeah, those government guys get all the high-tech crap. Probably some new fancy material that stops bullets and tear gas too. What the hell do I care? Let's go." He opened the door and walked out into the hall.

Pulling the door closed behind them, making sure it locked, Brad hurried to catch up to Wilkes. But he couldn't reconcile Bliss's appearance. An overcoat with unique fiber or treating might repel some water, but that didn't explain why Bliss's hair had been dry.

Chapter Twenty:

UNKNOWN LOCATION

The group had calmed down quickly, all things considered. Or thing. Singular. Fletcher's abrupt disappearance under other circumstances would have been shocking. But given the current set of variables, it had been shocking and scary, but not completely without precedent.

Jack watched the others assessed their reactions. Rafe seemed completely unaffected. Daniel appeared to be struggling with some guilt. Maybe relieved as well. Maddy was clearly shaken up. When Jack had asked her what they had been talking about just before Fletcher vanished, she said their conversation had touched on spiritual issues. Fletcher had been upset by his inability to get the rest of the group to confront Leiru. He also commented on his belief that a higher power was in control and that their current surroundings were smoke and mirrors. And then he wasn't there anymore. No pop, flash, or wisp of smoke. Just there. Then not there. Like the black woman earlier.

The fact that Fletcher and Maddy had been discussing a higher power at the same time that he had been having a similar conversation with Daniel and Rafe wasn't lost on Jack. There are no coincidences, he told himself. Sometimes you think you're headed in a particular direction looking for one thing, and you find something else.

It made him remember when he first felt involved with God but how he had lost that tenuous grasp on faith.

*****

When Jack was in his teens, his aunt had been fighting a serious illness. Countless trips to various doctors failed to yield a diagnosis, let alone a cure. Her vision had deteriorated, so she could only recognize shapes and light sources. At the same time, her motor control had suffered so badly that she couldn't feed herself. Walking was reduced to an interminable series of shuffling steps. Aunt Rose had not been a ray of sunshine during her prime, and illness had not done anything to improve her crusty and abusive disposition. In fact, it had distilled her surly nature to a sour, vinegary perfection of bitterness.

As Aunt Rose's conventional options dwindled, she turned to more esoteric solutions. Holistic remedies, superstitious rituals, and faith healers. Jack couldn't remember how many impostors claiming spiritual curative powers he had been dragged along to, but it had to have been at least a dozen. Some were famous, holding their events in sold-out auditoriums. Most were little more than modern-day snake oil pushers. It seemed to Jack that more women than men had been 'touched by God' and blessed with miraculous therapeutic powers. A desperate Aunt Rose once claimed to heal from dandruff at a revival.

They had left that particular event early.

Then one day, Rose seemed to experience a personal revival all her own. She made an effort to be pleasant. She said thank you. She stopped cursing and hitting.

Aunt Rose had found God.

Her inability to claim healing had been revealed to her. She hadn't accepted God in her heart. She had been chasing healing while wallowing in her sin and selfish ways. The

Almighty had come to her and spoken to her. He knew her heart, and she needed to repent, mend fences and humble herself before those she had wronged.

Jack, his cousins, and Uncle John had been skeptical at first. The behavior change had been so sudden and so...unlike Aunt Rose, it had been almost impossible to believe. But Aunt Rose maintained a softer and gentler manner for weeks. And then months. Uncle John thanked God for giving him back the woman he had married. Mick was happy that his father was happy. Mark was mostly noncommittal. New friendships were formed, and Aunt Rose would wax philosophically about the errors of her ways and the amazing cleansing she had experienced by accepting God.

Several times a month, Aunt Rose would ask to be driven to a different church so that she could bear witness to the power of the Lord. This was accomplished through casual chats after the service, by trading on her infirmity and getting the pastor to allow her time to speak before the congregation. Mick was usually her chauffeur for these excursions. Mark had commented once that he felt it was odd that these 'callings' seemed to coincide with the presence of a faith healer at the church destined to receive Aunt Rose's testimony. A hard right to his jaw from Mick had ensured that any other such musings would be kept in Mark's head and not on his lips.

One Saturday evening when Jack was around sixteen, Rose felt called to a small Pentecostal church in King City. Mick was unavailable because he had drawn a winning lottery ticket for elk season. Mark couldn't be counted on, and Uncle John had already gone to bed, so Jack couldn't pass the chore off when Aunt Rose asked him to drive her. While just sixteen, Jack had been driving for years. Hours of practice in pastures, dodging cow pies, and scrub brush, had equipped Jack with the necessary skill to navigate country roads behind the wheel of the family's dilapidated pickup.

The drive had been almost fun. The musty smell of ancient upholstery, cracking from too many days in the sun and heat, coupled with the sharp odor of oil and gas, was ambrosia to a teenager driving in the dark. Rose's newfound civility persevered, and the ride was quiet, save for the crackling of the radio, and the squeak of the truck's weary suspension.

The church was located far from the city and stood nestled in the middle of a sparsely planted walnut orchard. As they had walked up an uneven dirt path toward the steps of the entrance, Jack marveled at what looked like hundreds of coats of paint holding the small building together. Creaking under their feet as they ascended to the modest porch, the stairs showed the foot-worn discoloration of thousands of worshippers who had entered the doorway over the years. Exactly twelve pews, six to a side, were crammed into the interior. The aisle separating the rows was so narrow that parishioners on either side could touch hands should they be so inclined. Naked bulbs hanging from the crossbeams covered the interior with amber-colored accents. Moonlight filtered through cloudy windows set high in the walls, casting fleeting shadows on the roof's interior. Rose had encouraged Jack to find a seat as close to the front as possible. The tiny church, almost full and while they found seats in the second to last row, the distance to the podium that served as the pulpit was small.

It did not take long to recognize that the modest little church was home to a brand of charismatic worship that Jack had only heard about. Loud singing, wailing, and churchgoers speaking in tongues blended into an overwhelming miasma of devotion. Jack's head spun after the first hour, and he had chafed as Aunt Rose bore witness to what God had wrought in her life. And then, with the evening's services heading inevitably toward the spectacle of the guest 'healer,' the pastor approached the podium again. A smiling older man with a wisp of white hair encircling his head, he had thanked Aunt Rose for her testimony, raised his hands with palms out, and addressed his small flock. He spoke in an unhurried manner about the good news of salvation. As he related the story of God's sacrifice for His children, the pastor's voice grew louder and more powerful. He gripped the podium's edge with both hands, large ropey veins standing out on his sun-bronzed, work-hardened arms. Jack knew from experience what was coming next. Each time they attended services at churches that were welcoming individuals claiming the power of the Almighty, the church elders, and pastoral staff couldn't resist taking the opportunity for an altar call. Whether it was current church members renewing their faith, or guests making a fresh commitment to God, it was the icing on the cake. So to speak.

As the pastor prepared to invite people, a slender, middle-aged woman stepped beside him and touched his arm. After a brief whispered conversation, the pastor introduced Myra White to the congregation. Her exact age was difficult to guess, certainly older than forty but likely not over sixty. She was not overly tall but carried herself in a way that suggested power while still projecting humility. Jack had recalled having heard her name before. The newspaper recently recounted her travels through the Southwest. A tour that created some controversy because of her staff's claims about her divinely bestowed powers.

She had apparently requested that she be allowed to minister to those who answered the altar call. Graciously acceding, the wizened pastor stepped back and motioned Ms. White to the podium with a hand sweep. Before she could even beseech the parishioners to come forward, people were standing and making their way to the aisle.

Jack had managed to avoid the awkwardly conspicuous walk to the altar on other uncounted Church visits. He was bracing himself for the typical well-intentioned encouragement. Aunt Rose nudged him. Smiles and nods from people seated around him. His tactic was to ignore it by putting his face in his hands and leaning forward. To anyone looking on, it would appear that he was praying. He had congratulated himself many times on this simple maneuver and how well it worked.

But that night was different.

When Jack closed his eyes and leaned forward, he immediately felt many hands on his back and shoulders. When the hands did not pull away after Jack had stubbornly remained seated for a few minutes, he grew wary. This was not the way it worked in the past. When it became obvious, he wasn't getting up to answer the altar call, the hands were supposed to drop away and leave him alone. He had stolen a glance to his right shoulder, and although he could feel a hand there, he couldn't see one. Worried, he straightened up and turned to confront the owners of the pressing hands. But alas, there was no one there. The encouraging pressure had stopped, and the people behind them were calmly seated, sitting up straight with their hands folded or placed on their laps. They looked inquiringly at Jack, projecting innocence and ignorance of intrusive behavior. Jack turned around and resumed his camouflage 'praying' pose.

Within seconds the hands were back pressing relentlessly against his back and shoulders. Some were firmly pushing up beneath his arms, moving him out of his seat. Irritated and flustered, Jack stood up and turned around, prepared to challenge the rudeness of the offenders. Again, astoundingly, no one was leaning forward or in any posture, indicating that they had just attempted to push Jack out of the pew. Confused, Jack started to speak but couldn't find any words to address the situation nor the confused people behind him, who were now looking at him with concerned expressions.

'Do you need to answer the call, son?' asked one sweet-faced older woman.

Jack had shaken his head no and closed his eyes as he turned, preparing to sit down again. And the hands immediately came back. So firm and strong was the pressure that Jack found himself in the aisle before he could check his progress. Almost fearfully, he turned again, knowing he would find no one behind him. Upset and bewildered, he faced the front of the church as other people filled the aisle behind him. Ms. White stood at the podium with her arms outstretched, beckoning the people in line to come up. Her pale clothing seemed to glow softly in the dim light, giving the blond-haired woman an angelic appearance. She smiled directly at Jack, or at least it had seemed that way. And without willing it, Jack felt pulled toward the simple altar. His scalp tingled, and his limbs seemed as though they were miles away as he walked slowly forward. Unbidden, tears had flooded his cheeks. He shook his head, attempting to erase the entire scene from his mind to no avail.

When he finally reached the front of the Church, Ms. White had put her hands out to him. Trembling and unsure, Jack grasped one of her hands.

Unexpected heat and a mild shock had accompanied the touch. Jack gasped in surprise and then was swept into a fierce embrace by the Ms. White. His entire body shaking. Wracked with sobs, he fought to catch his breath through hiccupping coughs. Then slowly, she released him from her embrace, keeping her hands upon his shoulders. When she asked him if he was ready to accept God into his heart, he had heard himself say yes.

And he instantly dropped to his knees. Her hands were still on his shoulders; Ms. White looked into his tear-filled eyes and smiled.

'The Lord wanted you mightily, young man. He was after you the moment you walked into His house.'

The warmth from her hands was so powerful that it almost burned but did so without pain or discomfort. Jack had been dimly aware of applause, and voices lifted up in affirmation. He gathered himself carefully as he rose to his feet and moved aside for the next person. Ms. White gently pulled him back. Looking at his tear-streaked face, she smiled and said, 'The Almighty has planned some important work for you, Jack. Be ready when He calls.' And with that, her hands left him, and he walked unsteadily back to his seat next to Aunt Rose.

Aunt Rose waited until they were back in the truck, heading home, to ask about his experience. 'How did it feel, Jackie? I could hear people talking about you after the service. It must have been something special. Could you feel God's blessing come into you?'

Jack had been shaken to his core and found it difficult to talk about the experience. After several requests elicited short vague responses, Aunt Rose gave up and remained silent the rest of the way home.

The months following his spiritual experience were a hazy memory now. The fire burned in him immediately afterward. But things got difficult for him. The frustrating weeks when his friends looked at him like he was an alien. And then, Aunt Rose's newfound peace unraveled all at once.

She invited a pastor and his wife to the house for lunch. Afterward, she clumsily attempted to buy healing, explaining that she had heard amazing things about the pastor's church and the miracles there. She had visited several times but could not secure healing for her illness. She had convinced herself that a sizable donation would help 'seal the deal.' Embarrassed for her and slightly offended, the pastor and his wife quickly said their goodbyes. They departed without conferring any promise of healing for Aunt Rose.

The descent in her was rapid after that.

Aunt Rose hadn't even tried to hide her displeasure. Angry indignation gave voice to several ugly accusations focused on the pastor's honesty, sexuality, and fitness to lead a congregation. All attempts to dissuade her from that discussion were met with sharp rebukes. The profanity managed to return to her daily vocabulary, and the hitting returned as well. Now, spitting and feeble kicks were added to the repertoire. Uncle John resumed his stoic demeanor and buried his hurt in running the ranch.

Jack had been depressed. Somehow Aunt Rose's loss of faith, if she had ever really had any, took the shine off his own experience. It shouldn't have, but Jack's new beliefs had been fragile. He didn't have anyone close that could answer his many questions or mentor him. And so that bright time for him evaporated into vapor.

*****

Musing over his memories, sitting in the chair. Jack also wondered about the connectivity of Fletcher's comments and his vanishing. He wondered whether or not he had been looking at things from the right perspective.

It had been over a decade since Jack thought about his experience in the little 'Holy Roller' Church.

Were they being prepped to assist their captors or just being used?

Chapter Twenty-one:

SEATTLE, WASHINGTON

The drive to the station had been eventful. Wilkes was on his phone non-stop. Picking up bits of the conversation, he pieced together that Wilkes' captain had cooperated with a request from the NSA to turn over all evidence from open investigations related to anyone involved with the alley kidnapping. The FBI and the NSA were working together on several similar cases across the US.

Shifting his tall frame, trying to get comfortable in the small seat, Brad asked, "So where to? How are we going to figure out who told the NSA about Larry and everything else?"

Wilkes tapped his screen to end the call and dropped the phone in an open cup holder.

"We? Well, I guess that is the situation, huh... First stop is downtown. I've got that appointment with the woman who got left behind in the alley with you. And I think I know exactly who's been breaking ranks and talking to the government guys. But first, I need to jump on this interview before someone gets in the way of that too."

"I thought your captain was cooperating, handing over evidence related to the kidnapping. An appointment for getting a fix on Larry? She doesn't know him."

"Nah, not that. We're going to compare perceptions and see what comes out." Responded Wilkes, avoiding directly answering Brad's comment on evidence and disclosure.

"Ahh, you mean my crazy ID on the kidnappers? Didn't you already do that?"

Wilkes glanced over at Brad and smiled. "Oh, sure. But that was before you were making claims about where the bad guys might have come from."

Brad tightly pursed his lips and stared straight ahead through the windshield. Great. An opportunity to have the microscope twist back in my direction. "So, what about your boss's orders to turn over all information on the kidnapping?"

"Well, Mr. Mayo I'm going to let the fact that you were listening in on my conversation slide, seeing as how you're right here in the car and I invited you along, but I don't see this as ignoring the captain. I'm just trying to help." Wilkes's sarcastic grin belied that sentiment.

"Besides, if I turned over everything, that would mean suggesting that a task force visit Easter Island. Or Disneyland."

"Yeah, sure." Brad said.

Pulling into a newly refurbished garage off Stacey and Sixth street, Wilkes quickly found a parking spot, whipped the car in, hopped out and hustled to the elevator. He waved to Brad indicating he wanted him to hurry out of the car.

Brad followed him into the elevator and rode with him in silence. The elevator's interior didn't look like any of the typical rundown government buildings Brad had been in before. Glass and polished metal details were abundant. When the door slid back, it revealed a mezzanine that overlooked several open floors, all bustling with activity. Filtered sunlight streamed in through greenhouse windows all around. Taking long strides, Wilkes moved rapidly toward a spiral staircase at the far end of the sky bridge with Brad in tow. The air smelled of fresh paint. In fact, the whole place smelled like the interior of a new car.

Navigating through a crowd on the ground level and pushing toward a line of glass-enclosed cubicles, Wilkes stopped before one of the thick sliding glass doors and pressed his thumb against a fingerprint reader affixed to the door frame. After three seconds, the reader flashed to a glowing blue, and the door smoothly slid open. He stepped inside, waving Brad in behind him. A comfortable workspace with a desk, three chairs, and some sleek filing cabinets greeted them. A large computer screen recessed in the top of the desk was dark.

Brad took a slow look around the room examining all the details of SPD's downtown headquarters. Modern architectural features blended with technological elements in a decidedly non-governmental fashion. Dozens of holographic and glass touch screens decorated the walls. Multiple images shifted from one screen to another. Brad recognized several photographs that were associated with the Emerald City Vanishings.

"Wow. This is amazing. I always had envisioned you detectives huddled over some wood grain laminate table, surrounded by old, dilapidated metal filing cabinets."

Rolling his eyes, Wilkes sighed as he seated himself behind the desk and waved at one of the two chairs facing him, suggesting Brad take a seat.

"Up until six months ago, that's what it was. This is all new. It used to look pretty much like the station house where Fisher and I interviewed you guys the other night. That long fancy boardroom table in the middle, there is our new detective's table. Sort of a, what do you call it, homage to the old days. But now it's got computer screens embedded in the tabletop; the whole damn thing is plugged into the internet and connected to every other piece of equipment in the whole place. Since this Vanishing mess got big, this room has never gone dark."

"This looks awesome. Doesn't it help you? I mean, if all the data is immediately available, isn't that helpful with your investigations?" Brad asked.

Looking over Brad's shoulder, Wilkes could see Fisher making his way down the stairs. Raising a hand, he acknowledged him while he answered Brad. "Perfect example of the bureaucrats getting too far out in front of the curve. Most of our investigative information, CSI, forensics, case files, and field reports are still collected in the old-fashioned way. Converting all that stuff to electronic copies and filling out forms on a computer is still being figured out. Causes as many problems as it eliminates. Plus, we get to be in this fishbowl. Completely soundproof, but you can't even scratch your ass without everybody watching you."

Brad looked over at the long detectives' table in the middle of a community space at the center of the large, high-ceiling room. It was clearly a technological marvel. The detectives sitting at it were busy reviewing virtual paperwork, sliding forms and photos back and forth on the table. It was basically a giant touchscreen computer. Overhead, Brad saw monitors displaying street views throughout the city. Several depicted unruly crowds shaking signs. The demonstrations had been picking up momentum.

"I see the people are still unhappy with the plans for the statue. Progress moves at its own pace, huh?"

Wilkes snorted derisively, "progress? This place is some efficiency expert's idea of what a 21st-century police building should look like, with some help from a chain of command that's far removed from the day-to-day. They wouldn't have any idea of where to start in a traditional station. The new governor has been pushing every city in the state to modernize their police departments. And working on his pet project for the presidential statute no matter what the people think. He's a one-term governor, for sure. The mayor will probably run when he finishes his term."

"And where did they get all the money this?" Brad asked.

"The governor's relationship with the president seems to have opened the federal piggy bank for all sorts of project funding. But what does a lifer like me know, right?" said Wilkes as he moved a few items around on his desk.

Fisher walked up, making a show of tapping on the glass next to the open sliding door.

"Yo, partner." He eyed Brad with obvious curiosity. "And what's he doing here?" Nodding at Brad.

"Just doing a little follow-up on our initial interviews. You file the murder scene and start the book yet?"

Wiping his sweaty forehead, Fisher grimaced. "No. Should I still do that? Aren't we passing everything over to the G-men?"

"Yes, we still do that. We're just supposed to hand stuff over as we process it. We're not supposed to just hang it up. Are you okay? You look like..."

"I'm fine. Fine. I'm just kind of screwed up from that murder scene. I've never seen one like that, you know?" Fisher said, cutting off Wilkes mid-sentence.

Brad watched the pale and shaky detective shift his feet nervously while he talked with Wilkes. He wondered; just what kind of ugliness did Larry leave behind?

"Well, try to shake it off. I'd tell you to go home, but I need you here. I need to know that you're okay and that you've got your end."

Fisher stiffened up, glaring at Brad before speaking, "Yeah, I've got my end. You don't have to worry about me." He dropped a folder on Wilkes' desk, turned around, and went to another glass-enclosed cubicle two doors down.

Brad checked Wilkes' reaction to his partner's behavior. "Your partner seems a little pissed at you."

"Yeah, he does, doesn't he?" Wilkes watched Fisher's retreat until he entered his own cubicle. Taking a deep breath, he squared his shoulders and rubbed his hands together briskly. "We got other stuff to deal with; I'll worry about him later. Miss Cheyenne Johnson should be here any minute. I want you to wait in the office next door."

As he spoke, he reached for the folder Fisher dropped on his desk, opened it, and smiled. "Bernice, you're the best."

"What?" Brad asked.

Still smiling, Wilkes swiveled in his chair and placed a copy of National Geographic on a low bookcase behind him. He propped it up slightly so anyone sitting on the other side of the desk could easily see the cover.

Taking in the photograph featured on the cover, Brad frowned and said, "What is that for, Wilkes? Some type of investigation trick?"

"No, no tricks. Just a little visual aid for my chat with Miss Johnson." He smirked at Brad's obvious discomfort.

Leaning forward, Brad started, "Look..."

The computer screen in Wilkes' desk came to life, and a beep sounded from well-hidden speakers.

Holding up a hand, Wilkes said, "Hold on, this is probably our gal." He tapped a section of the screen and said, "Wilkes."

"You've got a Cheyenne Johnson signing in for an interview with you? You ready for her sir?"

Rubbing his hands together, Wilkes said, "Yep. Send her back." Looking at Brad, he said, "Look, trust me. Play along. I'm not setting you up."

A uniformed female officer approached Wilkes' office, escorting an attractive redhead. As they got closer, Brad recognized the young woman as the other victim of the alley mugging. Appearing unharmed, she was dressed in dark jeans and a cream-colored shirt that showed off her figure without revealing much skin. She carried a leather coat folded over her Meloney Brahmin purse.

The pair stopped just outside the doorway to Wilkes' office. The officer introduced Cheyenne Johnson and quickly left after being thanked by Wilkes.

"Good evening, Miss Johnson. This is Brad Mayo; he was just leaving."

Miss Johnson looked over at Brad as he stood up and walked out to another empty office. Her angular attractive features were lightly dusted with freckles. Taking a seat in the chair just vacated by Brad, she leaned back and crossed her arms over her chest as she asked, "So, 'hello' yourself. Have you figured out what happened? Are there any new developments?"

"No, we're just following up on our earlier line of questioning in an attempt to focus on any similar perceptions or descriptions of the events leading up to the attack."

Still appearing tense but less defensive, she uncrossed her arms and crossed her legs. She glanced around and then asked Wilkes, "Why was he in here? Don't you usually interrogate people separately? What is it exactly that you're looking for?"

Wilkes leaned back and spread his hands in an attempt to disarm her. "Miss Johnson, you are not a person of interest. This isn't an interrogation. I'm just interested in asking a few more questions to see if I may have missed anything during our first interview. You're free to leave at any time, but I would consider it helpful if you stayed, and it may help us locate your friend."

"You can call me Chey. It's easier than 'Cheyenne,' and 'Miss Johnson' makes me sound like a schoolteacher. Look, I want to help; it's just that this is so fucked up. Ohh, sorry. I meant messed up.

"It's okay. I just want you to talk freely. Don't worry about upsetting me with some colorful language," Wilkes said with a smile.

161

"Anything I can do to help find Maddy, you can count on it. I'm just having trouble processing all of this, you know. This is the kind of thing you see on the news or read about, but it doesn't happen to you personally. I mean, like, we were leaving work like we always do, and then...like, all of this happens. It's just too weird." She smoothed the material of her shirt with her hands.

She made a visible effort to collect herself, took a measured breath and said, "Well, what can I do? What else do you need to know?"

"I'd like you to take a moment and think back to the first moment you were aware that you were being attacked. Like, right before the actual attack. Where were you standing? Where were the assailants? How tall were they? How did you get a sense of their height? What were they wearing? Did you get even the slightest glimpse of their faces?" Leaning forward slightly, Wilkes rolled his chair to one side, improving the magazine's view from Chey's chair.

Looking first at her hands and then at the metal ceiling, Chey thought back to the events in the alley. Her eyes seemed to search the room for answers. She slowly lowered her gaze and shook her head.

"I can't think of anything that I left out before."

"That's okay. It will help me even if you cover the ground we've been over before. Start with the moment they came out of the alley."

Chey looked questioningly at Wilkes. "Haven't you already gone over all of this? Is there something you're hoping I saw that you already suspect?"

Wilkes raised his eyebrows. He didn't want to influence her recollection of the attack by telling her where his questioning was leading.

"Look, any two individuals who have experienced the same event will always have different perspectives. Remember different details. The scenery, smells, and everything gets its own personal spin. That's what I'm trying to get at."

Relaxing further, Chey uncrossed her legs, leaned forward, and smiled. "Okay. So...we're walking up the hill toward the bus stop, and then they were like, just...there. I mean, they didn't seem to rush out of the alley. I mean, they were...just not seeming to come from, like, way back in the alley. Like, they were maybe standing just inside the alley entrance, real close to the sidewalk. Except they were so huge and tall that if they had been that close, I would have seen them out of the corner of my eye. They...were so tall. I've been to basketball games and seen tall guys up close. But these guys were beyond that. They were fucking huge. I had to crane my neck back to look up into..." Chey stopped talking as she struggled to make sense of some memory or image.

Wilkes leaned toward her, "What? What did you look up and see?"

Mouth opening slightly, Chey fought to describe what she had seen. "They were, I saw...I saw he had this shape to his face. Like..." her eyes tracked erratically around the room and then stopped, "like..." Her voice trailed off as her eyes locked on the National Geographic magazine on the bookcase behind Wilkes's desk.

"Is that a joke?"

The cover photo prominently featured the monolithic heads of Easter Island.

Eyes narrowing, she glared at Wilkes.

Wilkes sighed, "No. It's not a joke. Let me explain how I'm trying to work this. Your help here is important to me. I brought the magazine in because of what someone else said during their interview. Does it mean anything to you?"

"Look man, I'm not interested in being laughed at or being called crazy based on your opinion of me or what I say."

Wilkes grunted and shifted uneasily in his chair. The fact that her speech had become less scattered and more articulate was not lost on him. "Does it mean anything to you Chey? Please." He indicated the magazine cover with a nod.

She looked at the magazine cover again and then back at Wilkes.

"What if it does? Does that tell you anything?"

"Maybe. It could potentially corroborate someone else's report of what went down in that alley."

She re-crossed her legs and stared hard at Wilkes.

"Yeah. It means something. The guys who mugged us looked a lot like that. Now what?"

Wilkes slumped back in his chair and rubbed his forehead.

"Well shit."

Chapter Twenty-two:

SEATTLE WASHINGTON

"Don't let it throw you," Wilkes told her. "Memories of events and descriptions can get muddled when a witness is under heavy stress." Still looking annoyed, she accepted Wilkes' card and promised to call him if she remembered anything else. He had explained to her that any details about the case should first be shared with him. After reassuring Cheyenne that she would be updated on new developments in her friend's disappearance, Wilkes told her she was free to leave. Her irritation and curiosity over the attacker's identification had been deflected by telling her that while her description was close to Brad's, there was no reason to believe that the assailants were anything other than human and that the SPD was still investigating leads.

Brad returned after Chey had been escorted out. Brad and Detective Wilkes sat across from each other in Wilkes' office. Casually flipping through the National Geographic, Brad said, "Hey, I guess I'm happy that she saw what I saw, but where does that leave us? You're not getting authorization or funding to take a trip to Rapa Nui."

Wilkes grunted, "Rappa Nooey?"

"Yeah. R-A-P-A N-U-I. It's the native name for the island. Polynesian culture. The stone heads are called Moai. Apparently, they're actually statues that include torsos and limbs, but many are buried up to the shoulders. So, there's the mistaken belief that they are just heads. Seems that one of the mysteries is how the statues were transported to their current locations. They're huge. One theory is that they came to life, and they walked to where they now stand or are buried. Another one is that aliens placed the statues."

Taking the magazine from Brad and putting it back into the manila folder, Wilkes said, "Whatever. I'm not sure what I was trying to accomplish. But it confirms what you said and leaves the door open for all sorts of bullshit if this story gets out."

He opened a drawer, dropped in the folder, and closed it. Hesitating, he took a handkerchief from his pocket, wiped the drawer, and pulled it open slightly. Glancing at Brad, he frowned and put the handkerchief back in his pocket.

"Gee, thanks Wilkes. So, you were still holding out on me, as in me being a nut case?"

"Get over it. The fact that you're here should be enough. Which is more than I can say for someone else in this building. Bliss and his agents couldn't have shown up as quickly as they did without getting some inside Information."

"Who...?" Brad started to ask when a beep announced another call coming through.

Angrily punching at his touch screen with his blunt fingers, Wilkes said, "hello."

"Detective, I have a call coming in from the Medical Examiner's office. Are you available?"

"Yeah, send it through."

A small chime sounded, and another voice emerged from the hidden speakers. "Hey? Wilkes?"

Looking at Brad with a finger held to his lips, Wilkes tapped another section of the computer screen. "Yeah, Wilkes here. Who is this? Martin?"

The voice on the other end made a throat-clearing noise, "Yes, it's me. Listen, we've got a problem with the body."

"What body?" Wilkes said with a firmer tone.

"The Ellsworth body."

"Problem, what kind of problem?"

"Uhm, I'm...can you come over here? I'd rather not discuss this on the phone."

Opening a drawer, Wilkes pulled out a small earpiece and placed it in his ear as he hit another colored button on the touch screen. "What is it, Martin? I don't have the time to fight traffic and come to you."

The conversation continued with only Wilkes' being audible to Brad.

Wilkes' face turned red, "What?!"

Wiping his forehead Wilkes started shaking his head violently side to side.

"No, no, no...you have to be fucking with me right now. Is it the Feds? No? Then where did it fall apart, Martin? All of it? You're telling me nothing is left...Who had access? OH, really? You think you're in trouble now; wait until Captain Galbraith gets through with your boss. We're supposed to be giving everything that's been processed to the NSA and the FBI. What do you expect me to tell him?"

Pushing violently away from his desk Wilkes stood up and started pacing.

"Alright, Martin. I've heard enough. What about your notes? Well, that's something. Make a hard copy and save all your electronic data on a drive. I'm coming over there right now."

Tearing the earpiece out and tossing it on the desk, he grabbed his coat and started pulling it on.

"What's happened?" asked Brad.

Pausing to take a deep breath, Wilkes looked at Brad as though just remembering he was present. "Crap! You've got to go. I'm headed to the ME, and you cannot come."

"What happened, Wilkes? What's going on?" Brad asked as he stood up and put on his coat.

Propping himself up with one hand on his desk, shaking his head again, Wilkes stared at Brad, "Our wonderful Medical Examiner has managed to fucking LOSE Natalie Ellsworth's remains."

Chapter Twenty-three:

UNKNOWN PLACE

"Hey Jack. Jack! What do you think?"

Jack dragged his thoughts back to the present and looked at Maddy. They were seated on one of the couches closest to the table of food.

"Hmmm? Sorry, what?"

"I said are we going to get together when we get back? Back to Seattle. What do you think?"

"Yeah, I'd like that. That would be good." He had was only halfway listening and tried to figure out the context of her comment. Is she talking about getting together romantically?

"To talk, you know? Try to put all this together. I mean, let's hang out and all. But don't you think we should try to make some sense of this when we get back? Or were you planning on just forgetting about it?"

Embarrassed, Jack smiled at her and said, "Yes, yes, and no. But, yeah, I agree, we need to keep in touch and figure out a way to study what's happened. You know and figure out how it connects. We'll need to call our friends and see what they've been going through. For all we know, they've been abducted too. They could even be in another part of this ship, place...or whatever it is."

"Oh, Chey! I'd completely forgotten about her. I don't even know what she's been dealing with. I hope she's okay. You said your friend was hurt badly, right?" She said as her smile went flat.

"No, I don't know. One got hit, and the other one got shot. But Daniel and Rafe got shot too, and they seem to be fine. I'm assuming that my friends are probably okay, too, physically. I'm just concerned about whether there's any fallout because of our kidnapping. Then there's our status to be concerned about. I'm guessing that Fletcher's disappearance might mean that we're all scheduled to be out of here soon. Despite what Leiru said, I just figured we'd all leave at the same time."

"Yeah, me too." Maddy said. She paused, mulling something over. "If Chey and your friends weren't kidnapped, they might have more information on what happened. I would guess that the police got involved."

"No question about that. I dialed 911. They had to have been there within minutes of us being taken."

Daniel and Rafe walked up, each munching on a piece of fruit.

"Private conversation?" Daniel asked.

Jack looked up, "No. We're just talking about what to do after we leave. You know, when we get back. And with Fletcher leaving, how we should be prepared."

Rafe nodded, "Yeah, not that I like it here, but this hasn't been awful either. How would we get ready for leaving? That looks like a surprise. It's a you're just gone kind of thing. There wasn't any warning when Fletcher evaporated. I just hope I have a job when I get back."

"Oh, crap!" Maddy gasped. "I was supposed to cover a shift...like yesterday!"

Rafe looked at her blandly, "Chances are good that you'll be fine. Kidnap victims aren't usually fired for not showing up. Me though? My boss is a jerk. I'm probably screwed. Although, I was on the phone with emergency when it happened. And then there's the fact that my door was smashed in. Maybe that'll save me."

Daniel took another bite of fruit and said, "I'm probably SOL. The only witnesses to Fletcher and me being taken were unconscious when it happened, and I doubt they'll be calling the cops to report it. I just hope my tutu is okay. She has got to be freaking out. People just don't disappear from an Island. Unless they're dead."

"How do we get a hold of the two of you?" Jack asked. "Maddy and I were planning on keeping in touch when we get back. We should know how to reach both of you too."

Rafe shrugged and sat in a nearby chair, "I can give you my cell number. I must have dropped it when they took me. I hope it's still there cause I can't afford another one. Maybe Leiru and Healer will give us new ones, huh?"

Maddy rolled her eyes, "Funny."

"Seriously," Jack said. "Give me your number. I think it's important that we all stay in contact. I'm kind of bummed about Fletcher. We should have been talking about this earlier. We don't have a way to get a hold of him."

Jack got up and walked over to a chair where he had tossed his coat. Fumbling through his pockets, he fished out his cell phone and returned to the others. Maddy already had her phone out and entered Daniel's and Rafe's numbers.

"No phone," Daniel said as Jack looked at him, waiting for him to pull out his phone.

"Beach. Remember?" Daniel said, grinning at Jack's reaction.

"Oh, yeah. Right. So Maddy and I are going to have to call the two of you since we're the only ones with phones and we can save numbers. Unless you guys are good at committing stuff to memory."

"Nothing to lose by trying." Rafe said.

"Fire away." Daniel said with a shrug.

When Jack finished entering the last number, he turned off the screen and said, "there's something else we should be doing too."

"What's that?" Maddy asked.

"We need to make up a story. A consistent way of explaining where we've been and what happened. Leiru warned about giving out too many details, and if we start telling people what really happened, we're either going to be shipped off to the mental hospital or end up on some History Channel documentary as 'lunatics-of-the-week.'"

"What do you suggest?" laughed Daniel.

"I think the simpler we keep it, the easier it will be to keep our stories straight. We don't remember, or we were blindfolded and never saw anything, something like that."

"Well, how about this," Rafe said as he looked at his shirt. "We were unconscious the entire time we were gone. Whatever, whoever knocked us out hit us so hard that we were out the whole time? And the first thing we remembered was waking up wherever it is that we will wake up. That would mean calling the cops or whoever as soon as we get back."

"Is that what I'm supposed to tell my parents?" Maddy asked. "They've been worried sick, I'm sure, and that's all the explanation I'm going to give them?"

Jack touched her shoulder lightly and said, "That's up to you, but everything you share with them has the potential of leaking out. Besides, how are they going to feel about an alien abduction story and any of the details about our time here?"

She made a face and sighed, "Yeah, you're right. I just feel bad keeping stuff from them."

"So, what are we agreeing to?" Daniel asked. "Knocked out, I don't remember a thing, is that it?"

Rafe cracked his knuckles loudly, "Sounds like the easiest thing to do. I have enough problems without making it worse by claiming to have been abducted by ET."

Daniel looked at Jack and said, "Jack, I think we should all do more than just get in touch with each other. We should figure out how to meet. All get together somewhere. I can get a cheap ticket through my cousin and fly to anywhere on the west coast. Since you and Maddy live in Seattle, maybe that would be the best place to meet."

Glancing at Maddy first, Jack responded, "Yeah, I guess. But each of us is going to have personal stuff, job-related stuff, to work out immediately after we get back. So maybe a couple of days after we get back? What do you think, Rafe?"

"I'm going to be the least flexible out of the group. I don't have much money. If I still have a job when I get back, I'll probably have to work to make up the time I missed."

"Time you missed. You were kidnapped, for fucks sake! What kind of an boss would make you work extra hours to make up for that?" Maddy said with her mouth open in disbelief.

"Hey, I'm not on a salary, I'm hourly. You don't know my boss. He's an asshole. Like a real special type of asshole." Rafe replied sarcastically.

"So, you definitely need at least a few days to get that sorted out. I agree with Daniel that we should all get together after we get back. We should play it by ear, then. Maybe we should all work around your schedule." Jack said while looking at Rafe.

"I mean, I don't want to be a pain, but I don't want to be left out either. Does that work for everybody else?"

Maddy and Daniel nodded their agreement.

Jack suddenly leaned back and slapped his hands together, "Fletcher! If we share our stories with the cops or family members, claiming to remember nothing of our abductions, and Fletcher gets interviewed or shares what really happened, we could be setting ourselves up for a problem."

Shaking his head, Rafe said, "No, dude. That's not going to be a problem. First of all, Fletcher is the least likely of any of us to allow himself to look like crazy. Second, his dad is wealthy, and Fletcher has some important jobs in his dad's company. Papa Blue Blood isn't going to allow any sketchy information about his son's abduction to get out."

Jack looked at Maddy and Daniel for their reaction. Both raised their eyebrows and shrugged.

"Okay. Okay, hopefully, that's how it will go. We really don't have any control over it, so we'll just have to see what happens." Jack said.

The group fell into a thoughtful silence, each considering what returning to their normal lives would mean and when it might happen.

"Hey, keep it down, everyone. It's a little loud in here." Rafe chuckled.

Jack appreciated Rafe's knack for lightening the mood. "Funny, isn't it? It's like we've talked ourselves out. I'm so tired of repeating details and trying to fill in the blanks where our hosts are concerned."

"Then what we have to tell you will be good news."

All four whirled around to see Leiru and Healer standing behind them. They had been so engrossed in their discussion that they hadn't noticed the door open or their entrance into the room. Healer stood silently behind Leiru, his height, and form no less daunting than the last time they had seen him.

Maddy stood up and faced them. "So, what's the good news? Are we out of here?"

His face serious, Leiru nodded, "You are indeed."

The others stood also, and Rafe stared at Healer.

"Holy crap!" Rafe gasped. "They said you were big, but damn!"

Healer approached Rafe, who shuffled backward.

"I will not harm you." Healer said. He stopped in front of Rafe and placed his hand on Rafe's chest. Rafe tensed but did not move away.

"Your healing is complete. Your body and your mind are cleansed of all the toxins they contained. You will feel no need of those things any longer."

"What?" Rafe asked. "I'm not gonna crave beer anymore? I don't particularly like someone else deciding what's good for me."

The others looked on uncomfortably. Healer stepped back and said, "Your choices are yours, as they have always been. I merely removed the wants you felt for poisons."

Leiru looked up at Healer and said, "The others? Are they well also?"

"There is no need to inspect them. They were mended when last we spoke." Healer said as he looked down at Leiru, who, although small by comparison, was clearly the superior.

"What happened to Fletcher? Why was he taken?" asked Daniel.

Leiru turned to face Daniel, "Do not fear for him. He is fully healed and prepared. He was sent ahead of you because his role precedes yours. As to whether he elects to accept it is up to him. He had reconciled his position as best he could, and no further time here would have changed that. The rest of you will leave now. There are others to prepare."

"How long have you been doing this? Are we the first? Is there a specific number of people you need?" Jack asked, feeling desperate.

Leiru looked at him kindly. "No more questions, Jack. Time for all of you to leave. You aren't the first nor the last, but you are special to us."

Healer stepped toward Jack, placed a massive hand on his shoulder, and stared silently at him. He finally squeezed his shoulder, turned, and walked back toward the doorway.

Rafe nudged Jack and whispered, "Well, at least you're special."

Ignoring him, Jack addressed Leiru. "That's it? Sorry about snatching you; you're all better now, and see you later?"

Leiru reached into the folds of his clothing and removed the familiar black stone.

"No, Jack, that is not all. Take this. The Orphan will protect you if given the opportunity."

He stepped forward, grasped Jack's left hand, and placed the stone in it, folding Jack's fingers over it. Then took a step back and raised his hands.

"Wait! Wait!" Shouted Daniel. "Do we all have to go back to where you took us from?"

Leiru paused, "No."

Daniel looked at Jack, "You okay with having a temporary roommate?"

Looking at Leiru, Jack asked, "Is that possible? Can you put each of us back anywhere we want?"

"Yes, anywhere, but decide quickly."

Looking at Daniel, Jack said, "I'd like to end up back in my apartment, and you're welcome if that's where you want to start from, man."

"I need to be back home with my folks. And my sister." Maddy said while looping her arm in Jack's. "But I want you to call me."

"Wow. I guess I'll just go back to my grimy apartment with the new doorway." Rafe said, shaking his head.

Leiru raised his hands again and looked at each of them, "Be well and..."

"What is this place?" said a voice behind the small group.

Turning, Jack saw a slender middle-aged woman with blond hair standing among prone figures.

Eyes wide with shock, he gasped, "Ms. White?"

"...be watchful." Leiru finished.

And the four vanished.

Chapter Twenty-four:

SNOHOMISH, WASHINGTON

Stretching his hand and placing it flat on the table, Larry looked distractedly at the pores in his skin. Beads of sweat slid down his forehead, nose, and dropped onto the table's surface. He traced a finger through the sweat puddle. The gas lantern suspended above the table swayed slightly, casting changing shadows across the walls and floor. He had been in the room for over an hour. Having spent the first fifteen- or twenty-minutes pacing about the windowless space, he surrendered himself to the chair, which, like the table, was securely bolted to the floor. Both appeared to be constructed from the same cheap plywood used to build the walls, floor, and ceiling. He had already concluded that if the room were under electronic surveillance, it must be disguised exceedingly well. It was obviously a room designed for interrogation. Still, it lacked the cliché two-way mirror, the grimy acoustical tiles, and the typical door with a small window. Instead, it was made from rough-grade plywood, small to the point of making him feel claustrophobic and completely featureless except for the light and the door. It also appeared to be newly constructed. The smell of fresh-cut wood filled the stuffy air, and sawdust was visible in every corner.

The ride there was terrifying, then boring. His head was covered in a black sack the entire time. His escort, or captors, hadn't offered any conversation. Larry didn't feel compelled to break the silence either.

Still hooded, he was forcefully walked from the car into a building and to this room. They finally removed the hood once securely inside. The two agents he'd been herded by, Dent and Slater, left the room without a word and locked the door behind them. Larry knew it was locked because he'd tested the cheap knob half a dozen times.

He didn't know what to expect but he figured It couldn't be any worse than where he'd been headed before Bliss, and his henchmen showed up. He made another mental note to figure out a way to thank Brad properly for setting him up. Although maybe that had actually been lucky, considering the detective that came on behalf of the police. What was his name? Wills? Mills? What a loser.

But opportunity or no, Larry couldn't fathom where this was going. Why the remote location? Why the secrecy? And most importantly, why come to his rescue and take him away from the cops?

The last few days had been unbelievably complicated, unprecedented, and Larry felt drained. He couldn't remember the last time he had slept, but electric flashes seemed to pulse through him. Somewhat painful and disconcerting. Like riding a rollercoaster in the dark. What it meant and what came next might be unknown, but Larry tried to remain calm. He felt he had to wait it out. Something big was coming. He could feel it. The whole Natalie thing could get sorted out if he was careful. He felt certain.

More time went by, and then, with no preamble, the door opened. Bliss walked in gracefully and unconcerned. He entered alone and left the door open behind him. To

Larry's surprise, the door opened directly to outside. He was grateful for the fresh cool air that rushed in.

Moving in an unhurried manner, Bliss walked over to the table and stood on the side opposite Larry. His clothing was unchanged from what he had worn earlier in the evening, but he appeared to have recently shaved. He looked fresh, rested, and entirely sure of himself.

"So, Mr. Ellsworth. What are we to do with you?"

Running a hand through his greasy hair, Larry grinned up at Bliss while he allowed himself to slouch back in the chair. "What? No chair for you? Would you like mine?"

Bliss smiled thinly and without hostility. "No. I prefer to stand. So, I'll ask again, what should we do with you? Dispose of you or make use of you?"

Larry spread his arms wide, feigning surprise, "Aren't we skipping something? Aren't you going to question me? Isn't that why I've been sweating in here?"

Eyes hooded and unreadable, Bliss moved closer to the table, "That is hardly necessary, Mr. Ellsworth. We have all the facts that we need about you and what you have been up to. Your useless role in the alley attack, your childish indulgence in baiting the police, and the unpleasant business you conducted with your wife."

"Don't talk to me about my wife about piece of shit! If you wanted to hang anything on me, you sure as hell didn't have to drag me all the way out to wherever we are. Not that I agree with anything you just said. Especially that crack about being useless. I would have liked to see you, or your primates deal with those monsters."

"I do not have the time nor the desire to exchange words with you, Mr. Ellsworth. And I'm far from being interested in punishing you for your behavior. It is your role as a witness to the kidnapping that causes me to consider you as potentially useful. My dilemma is to decide if you can be adequately controlled. I say controlled because you are clearly not trustworthy. As to your adversaries the other night, rest assured, if I had been present, the outcome would have been decidedly different."

Locking his hands behind his head, Larry chuckled lightly, "Really? Easy for you to say now. But you're right about one thing, it doesn't make sense to play games. You have something definite in mind, and I don't want to end up talking with the cops again, so I'll bite. What do you want?"

Moving closer so that the overhead light glowed down on his face painting it with deep shadows, Bliss spoke slowly, "Want? We have you. Everything about you, everything you do and own, is ours. I do not need to ask you for it. I already own you. You still don't understand. I see potential usefulness in you. But, if I am unimpressed at the end of our little discussion as to your suitability, then you will die in this little room. Quite painfully I might add. I will require your willing cooperation as I don't like variables. Perfection is in the details. Like the details you left carelessly lying about when you left your home this morning. Details we took care of. I don't like a mess."

Tendrils of nervousness crept up Larry's back, and the beginnings of uncertainty nipped at the edge of his confidence.

Glancing at the open door, he said, "What's to keep me from making a break for it? Are Goon One and Goon Two waiting outside to shoot me?"

Bliss frowned condescendingly, "Do not flatter yourself. While my associates are close by, I require no assistance dealing with you." He swept an arm toward the open door, inviting Larry to leave.

Swallowing involuntarily, Larry said, "I'm in no hurry. What do you require from me besides my cooperation? As you pointed out, I don't own anything you can't reproduce."

"Not wise but savvy, Mr. Ellsworth. I'll need your cooperation to make use of the relationships you possess. Relationships are power, but I'm sure that a powerful stockbroker such as yourself knows that. It's not what you know but who you know. Isn't that the saying?"

Larry silently nodded yes.

"But let's be clear. Cooperate and follow directions precisely; we will make your immediate problems disappear. And there will be rewards. But I will decide what they are and when they will be conferred. Continue your inclination for insolence with me, or disobey orders, and I will dispense with you in a way that would make your late wife's passing look mild by comparison."

Larry was silent. Fresh beads of sweat that had nothing to do with the temperature in the room broke out on his forehead. The cocky self-confidence of moments before wobbled and teetered like a child's top nearing the end of its spinning journey.

Clearing his dry throat and working to control the tremor in his voice, Larry asked, "What specifically do you want me to do? Sir."

Leaning forward, hands clasped behind his back, Bliss' gaze bored into Larry, "Whatever I tell you to do. Immediately, without question, without hesitation, and without fail. Because I only allow failure once from one of my subordinates. I require complete and precise execution of every order."

"Well then, I guess I'm your guy."

Bliss said softly, "Don't guess, Mr. Ellsworth. All or nothing."

Placing both hands on the table to keep them from shaking, Larry said, "No guessing. I'm in."

Bliss smiled without any warmth. He stared at Larry in a calculating way.

"Good. I believe we understand each other perfectly." Turning to the doorway, he called out, and the two agents came into the room carrying two wooden barrels and two large paper sacks.

Dent and Slater opened the barrels with knives, working quickly and without speaking. They began splashing the liquid contents of the barrels out onto the floor and walls. Acrid fumes quickly filled the small room.

Eyes opening wide in alarm, Larry attempted to jump up from the chair. With deceptive speed, Bliss was at his side instantly and placed a hand on Larry's shoulder, keeping him seated.

"Wait, Mr. Ellsworth. The show is just starting."

Slater and Dent emptied the barrels and proceeded to rip open the bags. Shaking their contents over the liquid, quickly soaking into the floor. A sharp odor joined the already thick air.

Bliss continued to press Larry into the chair. "This evening is a tedious but necessary example, for you, of how we work and execute our business. The liquid is an organic fuel made from chicken manure. The powdered chemicals are a combination of lye and sulfur. Together they will completely burn down this building without any evidence of artificial accelerants that are easily detected post burn. The fire will last less than an hour. Tomorrow this field will be plowed. The field workers will see the remains of the fire and assume it was one of many bonfires set by local teens celebrating whatever they usually do. Within a few days, well before an investigation of this remote field can be mounted, any evidence of what transpired here will be beyond forensic reach."

Turning to the agents who had completed their task, Bliss said, "Bring in the lady of the house."

The two men left and quickly returned with two misshapen and stained burlap sacks, dumping them onto the table. The smell made the hair on the back of Larry's neck stand on end, and he involuntarily shrank away from the bags. A twinge of vomit began to creep up his dry esophagus.

Bliss smiled grimly, "Ah, the late Mrs. Ellsworth. Family farewells are sometimes difficult. Would you like to see your bride before we leave, Mr. Ellsworth?"

The cloying rotting odor filled Larry's nostrils. All attempts at bravado now abandoned, he hissed, "No!"

Bliss chuckled, removing his hand from Larry's shoulder, "Well then. We should be off." He walked toward the door, followed by Dent.

Slater pulled a book of matches from his coat pocket, striking one and lighting the book, creating a small torch. The flames reflected on his blank face. Tossing it into a corner, he turned to follow Dent and Bliss.

Larry rose unsteadily; terrified and shaken, he felt overwhelmed by the malevolent presence in the room. Flames quickly climbed the wall and fanned out over the ceiling.

Looking back over his shoulder, Bliss said,

"Come. Let us begin our business together."

Don't miss out!

Visit the website below and you can sign up to receive emails whenever Chad Wannamaker publishes a new book. There's no charge and no obligation.

https://books2read.com/r/B-A-NUSN-REOKC

BOOKS 2 READ

Connecting independent readers to independent writers.